THE SWAY

A Hidden Saga Companion Novella

Amy Patrick

Oxford South Press/June 2015
Cover by Cover Your Dreams
Formatting by Polgarus Studios

For my Hidden Honeys- the incredible readers who love my books and send so much encouragement my way every day! I hope you'll enjoy Vancia's story and this peek at her history with Nox and what transpired between her and Ava.

CONTENTS

Chapter One
Partners

Sometimes the more a person talks, the less you want to listen. Even when he speaks without making a sound.

"This legislation will lead to more jobs for the middle class—this country needs to move forward, not backward." Pappa's voice drones on and on, flowing from the surround sound system in our living room like the underground river in Altum. Slow. Deep. Never-ending.

I reach over and click the remote, and the image of his unnaturally young, unusually handsome face disappears from the big screen, the manufactured smile and slick speech replaced by soothing blackness and quiet.

"Why'd you do that?" Carter whips his head around to face me across the low table where we're working together, surrounded by piles of books and trays of snacks prepared for us by Edda, my family's chef.

I shrug, not taking my eyes from my laptop, continuing to peck away at the art history senior paper Carter *should* be working on as well. Instead, his eyes have been glued to the TV for the past ten minutes.

"It's distracting," I say. "And boring."

"It's not boring. It's awesome your dad's on TV all the time."

Finally I look up. "It was *awesome* when I was thirteen. Now—it's boring."

Carter throws his hands up in an exaggerated pose of surrender. "Well *excuse me* for being impressed, Miss I-Have-Mansions-In-Two-States-And-Had-Dinner-At-The-White-House. Some of us *country bumpkins* could listen to him talk all day."

I gesture toward the row of floor-to-ceiling windows that look out from the living room over our manicured suburban neighborhood. "Atlanta is hardly the country. And you're not a bumpkin. And you wouldn't be saying that if you actually *lived* with him in those two houses and had to *listen* to him talking all day."

Carter shakes his head, the light blue of his eyes matching the color of his frayed button down. "No. He's not like other dads." Rolling his pen between his fingertips, he looks up at the soaring cathedral ceiling, obviously searching for words to explain the unexplainable. "Your dad's so… so…"

I know it's the glamour at work, and like all the other humans in our sphere, Carter can't help himself, but still, his reaction to Pappa's televised interview is bugging me. It makes me feel sorry for my new friend. It makes me feel guilty.

I lighten my tone a few degrees, adding a note of humor. "You're *kind* of creeping me out here with the hero worship."

Now his gaze comes back to me along with a sheepish grin. "Sorry. Not being weird. You know I want to go into politics, so to me, he *is* kind of a rock star. I guess to you he's just 'Dad.'"

"Exactly."

Only he isn't.

Pappa adopted me five years ago after my parents were killed in a small plane crash. He doesn't feel quite like a father—I remember what a real father feels like—but I'm lucky to have him as a guardian. There aren't many people (especially among *our* people) who'd take in a stray teen girl and raise her as their own.

"Anyway, you're not getting any work done with the TV on. And we've only got a few days left to finish this. So get on it." I lift my hand and flip it, making a cracking noise with my mouth to approximate a whip.

Carter flinches and laughs, places both palms on the table between us, and drops his face to his knuckles in a reverent bow. "Yes, master."

I laugh along, but only weakly, as a sick twinge hits my stomach. I don't like the sight of him bowing to me. It's too close to what Pappa actually believes all the humans should be doing.

Of course, Carter has no way of knowing about that,

and he can never know. I'm not even supposed to have friendships with humans, much less confide in them.

Pappa would probably flip if he knew Carter was even in our house right now. But he insists on my going to school with them—public school of course—*man of the people* and all that politician garbage—so he'll just have to put up with it when I have a partner on a project. The school library where Carter and I have been working together closes at three-thirty, and I have no doubt Pappa would like me going over to a human boy's house even *less*.

"They're only interested in one thing, Vancia," he's constantly warned me. "And that's the one thing you absolutely must not give them. You know the consequences."

Oh, I know. Believe me, I know. How could I not, when it's been preached to me so often? *Our kind have one partner for life. Separation from that partner results in the mark—and a solitary life for eternity.*

Though eighteen is the age of bonding for us, we all get The Talk in early childhood because even before our eighteenth birthdays, if we choose to bond ourselves with someone, that's it. No take-backs. No oopses.

I glance up to check that he's working and can't help but smile at Carter's concentration face as he scribbles in his notebook. The tip of his tongue is in the corner of his mouth, and his light brown hair is flopped to one side, revealing cute little frown lines across his tanned forehead.

A sweet warmth spreads through my chest, and I pull my gaze away, forcing it back to the screen in front of me where it belongs. No point in looking. A human—like

Carter for instance, with his short human lifespan—would be a tragically bad oops.

* * *

I hear Pappa come in long before Carter does. Of course, he's calling to me in the Elven way, so Carter can't hear him at all.

Vancia? Are you home? Where are you?

In the living room, I answer without making a sound. *And I have company.*

Now he repeats his question, using his voice this time. "You home Vancia?"

I scoot further away from Carter as I hear Pappa's quick footsteps echo through the marble foyer, hurrying toward the living room.

He steps into sight, surveying the wide open, sunlit space, his eyes dropping to me and Carter sitting on the carpeted floor at opposite ends of the low wooden coffee table, our shoes kicked off, our school papers intermingling. From the expression on his face, you'd think he caught us half-undressed in a lip lock.

Both Carter and I scramble to our feet, and my heart stops at the look Pappa directs toward him. It makes me feel like throwing myself in front of Carter—like I'm taking a bullet or something, but I hold my ground.

"Hi Pappa. I didn't think you'd be home for a while. We saw you on the news."

"That was recorded," he growls, never taking his eyes from my project partner.

"Pappa this is—"

"Carter Fields." Carter steps forward with his hand extended. He's got stars in his eyes as big as our TV screen, but I'll give him credit. Most humans who find themselves face-to-face with Davis Hart, Senior Georgia Senator and Science and Technology Committee Chairman, are speechless for a few minutes. Maybe Carter's debate team experience is coming in handy. "It's an honor to meet you sir," he adds.

Pappa must be surprised as well because the frown drops momentarily, and he grips his hand and shakes it. At the appearance of Carter's charming dimples, my father's scowl returns.

A few monosyllabic answers later, my project partner apparently gets the *No Trespassing* message. "Well, I guess I'd better get going. My mom will have dinner ready soon. It was nice to meet you sir."

Pappa nods, and I come quickly to Carter's side, helping him gather his papers and books so he can stuff them into his backpack.

"I'll walk you to the door." Pulling Carter along with me, I speed-walk toward the foyer and open the front door to the view of a wide double staircase flanked by stately planters overflowing with blooms. At the bottom, in our circular drive, Carter's old Jeep looks sorely out of place parked next to my convertible Mercedes and Pappa's new Bentley.

"Sorry about the cold front back there," I say as we step outside together.

He blows out a whistling breath and nods. "An ice storm is more like it. He's different than he is on TV, huh? Does he always act like that when you have someone over?"

"I don't know. I've never had anyone over before." *Great.* That was stupid. Not only am I the weird art geek girl, now he knows I'm friendless as well.

Carter's puzzled expression warms into a pleased grin. "So, I'm the first guy who's been to your house then."

Not the reaction I was expecting. His flirty tone makes me suddenly aware of the humid warmth of the evening air. What does it mean? Does he talk like that to all girls or is it actually something to be worried about?

We've been working together after school on our senior project for about two weeks now, and what started out as awkwardness has turned into a fun daily exchange of ideas and jokes… and sometimes long, loaded glances. Or maybe they're only significant on my end.

I study his face, trying to calm my racing pulse and wishing I could read his thoughts. Unfortunately, that's one thing we can't do. Some of my kind can read emotions, which is pretty close, but I don't have that glamour. Mine is artistic giftedness, which is almost laughably useless. Reclusive artists aren't exactly the poster children for winning fans and influencing people.

I know Pappa would rather I had some really badass glamour like hypnotic musical ability, or acting or athletic prowess, so I could be groomed for celebrity and have a fan pod of my own, do my part to advance The Plan. I can almost feel his disappointment when he walks into my painting studio and looks around, as if he's thinking *What am I supposed to do with this?*

Like all of my people, I have the Sway, but mine seems rather weak compared to the others I know. Or maybe I just haven't tried very hard to convince people to think or do things they otherwise wouldn't. Another disappointment to Pappa, who is the *king* of Sway. He could convince a cattle rancher convention to go vegan.

It might be worth it to use whatever Sway I *do* have on Carter now—nip this in the bud—if there even *is* a *this.* But when I open my mouth to do it, I find myself unwilling to influence him after all, so I try subtle redirection instead.

"Usually when I *study* with someone, I do it after school in the library, like we've been doing. We can work there tomorrow again—I think we got enough done today that we'll wrap it up on time."

"I don't mind coming back here. Your old man doesn't scare me." Carter's face breaks into a sunny smile, showing me that he knows how ridiculous his tough talk sounded.

What he doesn't know is that he *should* be scared of Pappa. And he'd be terrified if he knew *how* old my "old man" really is.

Chapter Two
Promised

What exactly is going on here? Pappa's silent voice would probably raise the roof if he asked the question out loud.

I cringe and close the front door, hurrying to join him in the immaculate kitchen. Sliding onto a barstool at the granite-topped center island, I watch him pace and begin to sweat.

"Nothing," I answer, preferring to use human speech. Unlike the Light Elves, who don't interact with humans at all, Dark Elves do, and I've spent nearly my whole life around them, going to school with them since kindergarten. Sometimes I forget I'm not one of them. "Just school work. Carter's my partner, and we have a senior project due in a few days. We've been working on the visual art element at school, but there's no way to get the written part done during the school day. We have to work on it after."

Why are you speaking aloud? Are you trying to deceive me?

A fair question. When we communicate in the Elven way, mind-to-mind, it's impossible to lie, but I'm insulted anyway.

No. Why don't you trust me? I never disobey you. And there's nothing going on. Just school work. Happy now?

He gives me a long, searching look. *Why is your partner so attractive? Did you influence your teacher to be paired with him?*

No. She drew names from a jar. At his narrowed eyes, I add, *I know the rules, Pappa. Don't worry.*

He visibly relaxes. *Good. Glad to hear it.*

He goes to the refrigerator and pulls out a glass pitcher of saol water. When he turns back around, his forehead is wrinkled and his brows are furrowed. I know this expression—it's his I'm-the-single-father-of-a-baffling-teenaged-girl look. His eyes come up to meet mine.

You know I'm only concerned about what's best for you. I don't want you to be stuck with someone who's… so far beneath you.

I flinch at his snobby remark, but I shouldn't be surprised. He and his buddies from The Council are always saying things like that, though I doubt they've taken the time to get to know any humans very well. They're too busy courting their votes and making laws to govern them, influencing them to hand over their money… and their sons and daughters to be members of the fan pods.

Unable to help myself, I come to my friend's defense. "Carter's very smart, and he's really nice. Everyone at school likes him."

Mistake.

"You do have feelings for that boy!" Pappa roars, letting the pitcher hit the countertop with a bang.

He must *really* be mad, slipping into human speech at home like that. Real smart, Vancia. Way to go.

"It is absolutely out of the question—for all the reasons you so well know," he continues. There's a long pause, and something new enters his eyes. "And there's another reason. Perhaps I should have told you before, but you were only a child and not even thinking of such things... and I didn't want to scare you."

I sit up straighter. The granite under my forearms feels suddenly colder. "Scare me about what?"

Pappa gives me the same wide smile I've seen him wear at high-dollar fundraising events, the one he uses when he's trying to convince donors of what a great guy he is. "It's good news, actually." He reaches across the countertop and takes my hand. "You are promised to someone. You have been for a long time."

I blink several times, trying to remember how to inhale and exhale. "Promised?"

"Yes. Betrothed. Engaged. Promised in marriage. A very important marriage, actually. One that will ensure your future as well as that of all our people."

"Marriage?" I repeat, my thoughts and feelings twirling together in a sinking whirlpool. All his words after that one sounded hollow and unintelligible, like the voice of Charlie Brown's teacher on one of those holiday specials I used to watch on TV.

Now Pappa's wide smile turns into something resembling irritation. He withdraws his hand. "Yes, Vancia, marriage. You can't be completely shocked by this. You're nearly eighteen. You know that's the age of bonding."

"Yes, but…" I'm already engaged? I haven't even… dated, or whatever. "Who is he? Do I know him?"

Now the see-what-a-great-thing-this-is smile is back. "No, you've never met. But I have no doubt you'll approve when you meet him. He's an excellent match for you. His father is the leader of another clan. So, you're marrying, in essence, a prince. I thought you might like that, as much as you enjoy reading those fairy tales of yours. We'll be travelling to Mississippi as soon as school is out for the summer. You'll be married during the Assemblage. It will be quite the grand occasion."

"I'm getting married in Altum? This summer?" All I can seem to manage at the moment are dumb questions.

I travelled to Altum, the traditional home of the Light Elves, ten years ago with my parents for the last Assemblage. Elven people from all over the continent had come together to trade, hammer out policy, and in general, have a hell of a party, as we do once every ten years.

I loved the opportunity to play with children from all the different clans, especially the Light Elves, who don't use spoken language at all. *They* reminded me of characters from my favorite books and fairy tales—so mysterious, hidden from human eyes, so close to nature and the ways of the First Ones.

Pappa and the other members of The Council don't hold

them in such high regard, calling them the Lightweights behind their backs and laughing. They think the Light Elves are stubborn and rather backward to ignore and avoid the human world and accuse them of trying to prevent the inevitable—the day when the Fae will rule the earth again as they did in ancient times.

"So, which clan is he from?"

"Actually he *lives* in Altum. His father is the leader of the Light Elves."

Again, I'm struggling to find enough breath to answer. "I'm betrothed to a *Light* Elf? But… you don't even like them."

He laughs out loud. "Of course I do. I think they're… quaint. A bit naïve perhaps. But they're fine people—especially your betrothed. And with some *convincing*, they'll see the light eventually. You will have a role to play in that. Once you've acclimated to your new husband, you'll persuade him to see reason, and we'll be able to share The Plan with them and get them on board. All our peoples will be united. It's a perfect arrangement, trust me."

Arrangement. *Arranged marriage.* The words spin through my head like Irish step-dancers. I'm going to be bonded to a boy I've never even met. Or perhaps we did meet as seven or eight year old children, but I don't even have a clear memory of the Light King, much less his son.

Arranged marriages are quite common among our people. With the age of bonding being so young and the bond being a forever one, it makes sense. You don't want to spend eternity with someone based on a hasty decision or changeable things like feelings and attraction.

But having spent my entire life around humans, reading their books and watching their movies and listening to their music, I'm finding the idea of a marriage without love rather... repellant. I never quite realized it before this moment, but I *want* that racing heart, that head-in-the-clouds, dreamy feeling I've read about and hear the girls at school describing.

The closest thing to it I've ever felt is for my book boyfriends, and before that, for my childhood best friend Nox. His parents were musicians, like mine, and we grew up together in Los Angeles, running around at rehearsals, entertaining ourselves as the grown-ups made music and shared the peculiar lifestyle of the music industry.

Around the time we turned twelve, my feelings for him changed from goofy, bickering, teasing friendship to a massive crush. *He* changed, too, becoming a tall, lanky, handsome pre-teen whose beautiful eyes and budding musical talent made my heart fluttery.

"I'm not sure," I whisper, the quiet statement seeming to echo off of every shiny surface in the kitchen. They're the first words of defiance I've ever dared to speak toward Pappa.

He gives me a disbelieving look. "What do you mean you're not sure? What is there to be sure about? It's been arranged."

My chin lifts, my eyes meeting his straight on. "I'm not sure I can... marry someone I don't know, someone I don't love."

He grunts and turns to pull two glasses from the cabinet behind him. "Love. What does all their *love* get for these humans? They divorce almost as soon as they get married. They bond with anyone and everyone who catches their eye. All they get is pain for their efforts. What we have is far superior to love." Setting the glasses on the counter between us, he fills them and pushes one to me. "You *can* marry him, Vancia. And you *will*."

His tone leaves no room for argument, and I drop my gaze, nodding weakly, though everything inside of me is thrashing like a two year old having a meltdown at the grocery store. Taking a sip of the sweet and slightly bubbly liquid does nothing to cool the angry lump burning in my throat.

"What's his name?"

Pappa studies me a long moment before answering. "It doesn't matter—you don't know him. But soon all will be revealed, and I promise you my daughter—you will enjoy living the life of a queen. You will see that I've done very well by you indeed. Now, dress for dinner. Our guests will be here within the hour."

Chapter Three
The Council

I drag my heavy silver fork through the beautifully presented food on my china plate, having no appetite for the four course meal served in our large formal dining room. Everything tastes fine, but I can't eat—unlike our two human guests, who are shoveling it in like they've never had anything so delicious.

Stifling a giggle, I turn away and study a wall mural of bathing nymphs under a fantastic starlit sky.

I have to remember the humans can't help it. Edda's culinary glamour affects them more strongly, just as other forms of glamour have a more powerful effect on humans than on other Elves. Maybe that's why Pappa invited the men here tonight for a meal. It's unusual for him to entertain their kind here, but nothing he does is random.

The members of the Council are here as well, posing as Pappa's friends. I suppose they are the closest thing he has to friends, though I wouldn't trust a one of them as far as I could throw them. Their lips smile and agree with Pappa while their eyes seem always to gleam with secret intent, as if seeking some new angle for self-advancement.

Like all Elven people, they are tall and elegant, the men improbably handsome, the women, beautiful and eternally youthful. Looking at them seated around the long dining table in their impeccable clothing, it occurs to me they could be Pappa's brothers and sisters, the resemblance is so strong. You'd think that would strike the human men as strange, but they don't seem to be fazed by it.

"Now, I'm not sure about that, Davis. What about the areas near schools? People get all up in arms about putting cell towers close by." One of our guests, a fifty-ish man who looks like he knows his way around a fundraising dinner table, is getting red in the face as he gestures with his fork, arguing with Pappa. I recognize him as a senator from the opposing party.

I tune back out of the dull conversation, which concerns the latest advances in cell phone and tablet technology and expanding signal coverage—pretty much all Pappa and his Council ever talk about. Tonight he seems to be trying to convince his fellow senators to change their positions and support a bill pushing more aggressive construction of towers and expanded wireless signals.

I have nothing to add, even if I were interested. Which I'm not. My mind keeps returning to Pappa's announcement and all its repercussions, which slam into me one after the other, making my lungs ache.

I'll have to move.

To Mississippi.

Rural Mississippi.

I won't see the people I've spent the past five years with at school anymore. I won't see my teachers.

I won't see Carter.

Now my lungs burn and threaten to close altogether, making me feel like I'm drowning right here in the perfectly dry, perfectly temperature-controlled room.

I'm not all that close to any of my human peers, but still, after being ripped so suddenly from my childhood home in California, there's a certain comfort in the familiar faces and the routine I've developed here. I much prefer our Georgia home to our place in D.C., where I don't know anyone except our servants.

I guess I won't be going to art school either, though it's secretly become a wish of mine over the past few months. Listening to the other students talk about college entrance exams and essays, applications, and weekend campus visits, I began to entertain the idea of going away to school myself, researching them online and halfway falling in love with one or two.

Higher education isn't the typical path for our kind, but I've been crafting the arguments for it in my mind recently. *I'll work on strengthening my Sway, and I'll influence other art students. I'll become a famous artist and have my own weird artsy fan pod.*

I knew all along it was probably a futile dream. Now there's no chance at all.

"Well, you are one convincing man, Davis. You can count on my vote," the graying senator says as he pushes back from the table twenty minutes later, the plate and wine glass in front of him empty, his belly protruding a bit further over the waistband of his slacks, his eyes glazed and peaceful.

"Mine, too," says the other visitor, a quieter man, but powerful within the Senate Science and Technology committee. "And give my compliments to your chef. I've never had such a meal." He stands and pulls on the jacket he'd draped over his chair back. "I hate to leave, but unfortunately, we've got to get to the airport."

Pappa rises and shakes each of their hands in turn, smiling widely. "It's been a pleasure having you in my home. I'll see you next week in D.C. and we'll push this thing through, boys." He's putting on the thick Georgia drawl he saves for special good-ole-boy occasions like this one.

The well-fed humans are obviously buying the act, smiling and back-slapping like old friends instead of his political rivals. I'll bet their constituents would just spit if they could see them now. My stomach turns sickly at the victorious glint in Pappa's eyes.

The minute the men are out of the room, satisfied laughter begins around the table, the musical sound more perverse than pleasant. Only the Council is left—its six members representing the inner circle of Dark Elven power on this continent. One of them, Thora, lives here in the Southeast. The others live in the West, North, and spread throughout the center of the country.

Though the conversation now is relaxed and jovial and

the saol water is flowing, I still don't join in. Being around the Council gives me the same feeling I get when the school nurse announces a lice outbreak—a sort of shivery, creeped-out, get-me-out-of-here reaction.

I'm not sure if it's their constant scheming, their disdain of humans, or just the Council members themselves, but the Elves Pappa chooses to surround himself with almost make me wish I *wasn't* Elven.

"… don't you agree, Vancia?" Audun, the Northeastern councilor is staring at me with penetrating light gray eyes that always make me squirm and question whether he *can* actually see my thoughts.

I've never seen human eyes like that—maybe it's all the centuries they've seen—maybe it's just a Fae thing. Audun's high cheekbones, dazzling smile, and blond curls give him a benevolent god-like appearance, but he's my least favorite Council member by far.

"Um, excuse me?" I say, fighting not to recoil from his intimidating gaze.

"He asked you about fan pod interest in the high schools here," Pappa interjects. "Do you think it's increasing?"

"Oh yes. Definitely. Pretty much everyone I know has applied for one or plans to."

Except for Carter, but he's not like everyone else anyway. He doesn't have a TV at home or a computer of his own. He works nights and weekends to pay for gas and his phone. But he's turned his impoverished background into a benefit. He's read almost every book in the school library and has the brains to show for it.

"Well, I know we can count on you to do *your* part," Audun says in that smarmy way of his, adding a knowing laugh as he reaches for his newly re-filled wine glass.

I nod and lift a forkful of food to my mouth, hoping it will remove my obligation to converse further. *My part.* Right. In addition to marrying a boy I don't know in the service of Elven unity, I'm expected to spend my time with humans being all "fabulous" and influential and talking up Elven celebrities and their fan pods, pushing my peers to join.

My natural Elven appearance is supposed to help in this mission, though I'm not sure the glances my unusual height draws are admiring ones. And if the Council—and Pappa—only knew what a social outcast I am at school, they'd probably yank me out and send me to the woods of Mississippi even sooner.

"What about modeling, like my Ava?" Thora suggests, referring to her flashy ginger daughter and nodding her own shiny copper curls toward me. "Several of our models are finding their fan pods to be quite popular. We need *everyone's* participation. We don't have the numbers we need yet, especially with the Lightweights refusing to participate. Ava's here for a visit, but she's flying back to Los Angeles next week." A delicate brow lifts toward her smooth forehead. "Perhaps Vancia could go along?"

A new light enters Pappa's eyes. "Yes, that's something that might work well for her. I'll talk to Alfred about arranging a portfolio shoot. She really should have a pod in place before she's married, and there's not much time left."

My face heats as the others nod in agreement, and the conversation about my future continues without me. Several of my Elven friends have moved to L.A. or New York recently to model. I guess if you can't sing or act or play sports with inhuman talent, at least you can look good wearing their designers' unrealistic ideas of fashion.

In fact, when I recently flipped through this year's Sports Illustrated swimsuit edition, I noted that most of the models were Elven. Feeling heavy with guilt, I deposited the magazine in the nearest trash can.

It seems rather sad to sell the Elven figure as the ideal to human women and men. It isn't attainable for most, and why should it be? But most Dark Elves see it as an effective way to gain human attention and adoration, and obviously it's working.

Pappa turns to me with an expectant grin. "You wouldn't mind a trip to L.A. for spring break next week instead of coming to Washington with me, would you darling?"

Ooh. He has no idea how tempting that sounds—a week without Pappa constantly looking over my shoulder. But there's a problem. "I have no idea how to model. I don't even like having my picture taken."

"You'll figure it out," he insists. "You're my daughter. You can do anything you want to do."

Of course, what he really means is that I'll do anything *he* wants me to, and we both know it.

CHAPTER FOUR
LIGHT

A touch of cadmium yellow—that's what it needs.

I smile to myself, adding delicate sun-dappled highlights to the swaying grasses of the meadow scene on my canvas. The art room comforts me with its familiar scents of paint and turpentine, the slightly burned tinge of freshly sharpened pencils. It's quiet. Only Mrs. White and I are left in the room, and she's packing up her bag to go home for the day.

She stops behind me to survey the nearly-finished work. "It's beautiful Vancia—luminous—your best yet, I think. It should round out your portfolio perfectly." After a pause she asks the question I know is coming. "Send any applications yet?"

Without looking up at her, I respond with a quiet, "Not yet." I don't want to see the disappointment in her eyes. Mrs. White is my biggest cheerleader, and I know she doesn't understand my apparent foot-dragging about applying for art school.

She lets out a heavy sigh and her heels click across the tile toward the classroom door. "Don't forget to lock the door on your way out. See you after the break."

"Okay. Enjoy your vacation," I say, my words colored with guilt. I hate knowing I'm letting her down. I admitted my secret dream to her after she suggested I pursue art as a career. She's been so caring toward me, expressing such an interest in my future and my talent, suggesting schools for me. But her disapproval is nothing compared with Pappa's.

I don't have to live with Mrs. White every day and navigate her moods and whims for my survival.

At the sound of the door opening again, I glance up. "Forget something? Oh… hi."

Carter's shaggy head protrudes through the opening. "Ah, the artiste at work," he says, putting on a very bad fake French accent. "I thought I might find you in zee studio."

He lifts his phone, and the camera flashes in my direction.

"*What* are you doing?"

"Capturing your light." Coming into the room, he stands near the doorway and snaps another picture while I throw up a hand to hide my face.

"What are you talking about? All this art theory is going to your head, I think."

"No, I'm serious," he says. "You glow when you're painting. You have this little light inside you, like Tinkerbell."

"Someone has seen too many Disney movies—and it's

not me," I mutter, embarrassed but also pleased by his observation. I actually *feel* warm and glowing inside when I paint.

Carter strolls over to stand at my shoulder, one hand stroking his chin and one eyebrow raised over a stuffy pursed-lip expression. "C'est magnifique. A masterpiece." He lines up his camera phone again and takes a photo of the canvas. Then gesturing at the painting, he further slaughters the French language. "See how she uses zee elements of light and dark to convey emotion, zee internal struggle of all humanity expressed in pastels on canvas."

I laugh, elbowing his side with my non-paintbrush arm. "They're oils, silly, not pastels. And I only paint light subjects. I don't like the dark. I never even use brown or black."

"Other than that I was dead-on," he quips. Dragging over a nearby chair, he straddles it and leans over its straight back to face me. "So, you excited about heading to D.C. for break—cherry blossoms and all that stuff?"

"Um… well, actually I'm going to Los Angeles instead."

"Los Angeles? When did this happen? Dad got a big Hollywood fundraiser or something?"

My face heats as if being fired in the pottery kiln. For a moment I consider lying, but then decide on honesty with my one and only friend. "Well, this is going to sound kind of weird, but I'm going to have some pictures taken. For uh… modeling." Squinting my eyes and cringing, I wait for his response.

He bobs his head up and down, his bottom lip coming

out and in as he appears to think it over. "Yeah. I can see that. Cool. You're full of surprises, Van. I didn't even know you wanted to be a model—thought you were all into the artsy fartsy stuff." He gestures toward the paint pallet on the table beside him.

"I don't. I am. I mean, it's not my idea. It's my dad's. He knows an agent out there, and he's setting the whole thing up."

"Oh. So… maybe I'm missing something here, but why are you doing it if you don't want to be a model? Or maybe you really *do* want to, and you're being all modest or something?"

"No. I definitely *don't* want to do it. I just—I can't say no to him. It's what he wants… and I owe him."

His face screws up into a comical scowl. "You don't owe him. He's your dad. What—you do every single thing he wants you to do *all* the time? You're going to have to turn in your teenage rebellion card, young lady."

I laugh. "No, I mean, well yes, I guess I kind of do what he says all the time. You know I'm adopted. And… I guess I appreciate that he took me in when most people wouldn't have. And he probably does know what's best for me. I mean, he's practically running the country, right? He's pretty smart."

"Yeah, but big difference between making laws for the masses and planning someone else's future. For what it's worth, it's your life, and I think you should do what you want to with it."

If he's this impassioned about the modeling thing, what

would he say about the arranged marriage? I'll never know because I'm certainly not going to tell him about *that* mortifying turn of events. In fact, a change of subject is in order.

"What would *you* do if you could do anything?" I ask. He's registered for fall classes at a nearby junior college. He told me he'll live at home with his mom and keep working to pay for tuition.

He rocks the chair back then lets the legs fall to the floor again. "Anything? Easy—I'd play for the Braves. But since I struck out pretty much every time I ever got up to the plate in Little League, I'd say that's out for me." He chuckles.

Then his smile falls and he rests his chin atop his folded hands on the chair back. "Honestly, I'd get away from here—go to a *good* school, you know? Somewhere maybe up north or out west, somewhere nobody knows me or where I came from. And I'd work my ass off to be the top of my class and graduate in three years and get an awesome tech job—maybe Silicon Valley or something like that, make a fortune, run for President. Along the way, buy a cool car, a house or two."

The longing in his voice makes my chest tighten. "Why don't you do that?"

"You know why. Hey—your turn. What would you do?"

"If I could do anything?" My heart flutters at the idea of saying it aloud. But what's the harm? Pappa can't hear me here. I'm ninety-nine-point-eight percent sure Carter won't laugh at me. "I'd get away, too, go to art school, sell my paintings, buy a cool car and a house or two."

He laughs. "You already have a cool car and a house or two. But seriously, why don't you do that? I'd kill to have your choices."

I shake off his words. "Just because I have money, that doesn't mean I have choices. My *dad* is the one with all the money. *And* he makes all the choices. He doesn't like my painting. He says it makes me a recluse, and it's never going to go anywhere. He wants me to make a name for myself, like he did."

"I don't know. I don't buy it. A girl like you—I think you can do anything—and you don't need anyone. I mean, if money for art school is the issue, you could do both—model and make your dad happy, then take the money you earn and pay for tuition." He nods toward my bare legs. "That's what I'd do if I had stems like yours."

I gasp and swat at him, and he jumps back out of his chair, striking a cheesy modeling pose. "And those cheekbones." Another pose. "And pouty pink lips." Pose. "And a booty like—"

He lets out a cackling laugh, dodging as I leap out of my chair and go after him with a loaded paintbrush.

"Shut up, you idiot!"

Running toward the door and throwing it open, Carter whips around and backs into the hallway, facing me with his hands up in the surrender pose and laughter still in his eyes. "I believe that's an unauthorized use of school supplies. I gotta get to my job. See you after break, Tink. Have fun in Never Never Land."

He spins around and saunters down the hallway, loudly singing "You Can Fly."

Chapter Five
Wipe Out

I place the painting on an easel in my home studio, stepping back to survey the finished picture. It was probably stupid to carry it home before it fully dried, but I didn't want to leave it at school over break.

As Mrs. White said, it's probably my best work so far, and honestly, part of me wants Pappa to see it. Maybe he'll look it over and say, "You know, I can see it now—you're *not* wasting your time—you *are* meant to be an artist after all."

Right. And maybe the Hemsworth brothers are human beings and not Elven. Ha.

Ah—you're home. Why were you late?

Pappa's question makes me jump. He entered the studio without me hearing him.

I spin around to face him. "Just wrapping things up before spring break." Stepping to the side so the painting is no longer obscured by my body, I gesture to it. "I was finishing my latest piece."

He glances at it. "The meadow near the lake. Yes, well, it looks like it, I guess." Then he turns and heads for the door. "Don't waste too much more time in here. You need to pack—you have the early flight out tomorrow." And he leaves.

Hope drains from my chest like air leaking from a beach ball with the plug pulled out. Slowly I turn to face the painting again. In the afternoon light coming through the wall of windows, the colors appear even more vibrant than they did in the art room at school. The grasses seem to dance with their own energy, and I can practically smell the breeze across the meadow, hear the tiny insects moving among the spring flowers that dot the landscape.

I suppose it *does* "look like" the meadow by the lake near our home. Something any cheap camera could capture.

Crossing the room to the supply closet, I lift a can of white paint and a roller tray and carry it across the room. I pry off the lid and pour it, filling the well of the tray. Then I go back to the closet and find the tool I need. A roller brush.

As I dip the roller into the tray and rock it back and forth, a tear plops into the paint, raising a tiny splash. Lifting the brush, I roll it across the center of the canvas. Vertically. Horizontally. Diagonal slashes back and forth, up and down, until the meadow scene has disappeared entirely behind a wall of blank visual silence.

Some masterpiece.

CHAPTER SIX
QUESTIONS

They look so young. My mom. My dad. Though I know they would have appeared no different today, I still smile at the youthful images of my parents, the photos five years old now, and imagine them looking more mature, like the parents of kids at my school, like Mrs. White.

I touch my mom's image, my throat tightening with a familiar ache. She was beautiful. Well, all Elven women I suppose are technically beautiful, but to me she was especially so. My platinum hair came from her. She wore hers in its natural curls while I usually opt to straighten mine to better fit in with my human classmates. Her bright blue eyes smile at me as if to say *I approve of you. I love you just as you are.*

My dad was tall, of course. He seemed like an oak tree to me back then. Now, I guess I'd be only a few inches shorter than him. His loose chocolate brown curls frame his smiling face in this photo taken out by our pool in California. Carter would probably have been impressed with that house, too, if he could've ever seen it.

I haven't told him who my parents were—he might recognize their names from the oldies radio station and start asking questions. Questions are bad.

Anyway, I took Pappa's last name—his human one—when he adopted me shortly after their deaths. He was the head of the Council at the time, third in line to the throne, after Nox's father and mine. Obviously, he's a politician not a musician, but he knew my mom and dad well, just as he was close to Nox's parents, who died with them in the plane crash.

Sifting through the pile, I come up with a photo of Nox and me. We look about eleven in this one, maybe twelve. He towers over me, though we were the same age. His black hair shines in the bright sunlight as he grins and makes bunny ears over my head for the camera.

I was so mad at him after the photo was taken, and I turned around to discover his split fingers in the air behind me. I remember wanting that photo to be perfect, having just come to the realization of how much I liked him *like that*. I wanted a memento to keep with me, to look at in between our family get-togethers.

We lived on different sides of L.A., so we didn't attend the same school, and sometimes it would be weeks in between visits. I remember toward the end… before the crash… thinking I'd *just die* of longing before the next time I saw him. It had probably been only a couple of weeks. But now—now I've gone for more than five years without seeing him. And I'm still alive. At least on the outside.

Tears well up inside my eyelids and prick at my nose. I drop the photo back into the box, fishing out another one of our two families together. It's still hard to believe all of them are gone—wiped out in one terrible moment on a sunny Southern California day.

Studying my own tiny, smiling face in the photo makes me unspeakably sad—that little tow-headed girl, so carefree—has no idea her life is about to change forever. Because of all the people in that happy photo, she will be the only one to survive.

I scoop up the rest of the photos from my bedspread and reach for the tissue box on my bedside table. At the sound of a throat clearing, I startle and twist toward the doorway.

"I've come to say goodnight." Pappa steps into the room and comes to my bedside. "I thought maybe you were up here reading, but now I see… are you all right? You're crying."

I swipe at my eyes and blow my nose, shaking my head in a stupid denial. "No. I'm fine. I was just—I don't want to forget what they looked like, you know?"

"You miss them," he says, sitting down beside me on the coverlet. "That's natural. I'm sure no one feels it's time to lose the ones they love, but it's even harder for us, I think. It's unnatural."

Accidents and violence are the only things that can end Elven lives. Human illnesses like cancer and heart disease and even flu don't affect us. We age, but only to a certain point. At full maturity, Elves stop aging and stay the same in appearance and health and fitness for eternity. Pappa himself is more than two-hundred fifty years old, though he looks no older than thirty.

"Can you tell me a story about them?"

"Your parents?" Pappa shifts, looking uncomfortable, like he hates discussing death even more than I do, but he manages a small smile. "Well, I can tell you about the night you were born. Of course, you know your father was our leader and your mother our queen, so your birth was quite a big deal. A ballroom full of our people gathered at your parents' home once the word went out that the blessed event was imminent."

He pauses, but seeing my smile and nodded encouragement, he goes on. "Even the human media got wind of it, since your parents were famous musicians, and there were cars lined up around the block outside the gates of the estate. Your mother was attended by our physicians up in her quarters, and the house was quite large.

"But shortly before midnight, even over the music and noise of the crowd, we all heard your voice as you came into the world. You were so loud, it was as if you were in the ballroom with us. One by one, people started laughing. Someone next to me turned and said, 'That's some set of lungs. Another singer, for sure.'" Now Pappa laughs.

I give him a smile, like I know I'm supposed to, but I can't share his amusement. The story leaves me even more melancholy than before. I'm not a singer like my parents, much to Pappa's disappointment.

Was I a disappointment to them as well? I have vague memories of my mother praising my drawings and paintings and of my father hanging my artwork in his office, but I suppose all parents do that sort of thing.

Still, I never doubted their love for me. I *belonged* to them. I was part of a real family. And I had a true friend in Nox. The stupid engine failure took away everything and everyone I ever cared about. It seems impossible an event with such a devastating impact could be caused by something so stupid and random.

"I want to know about the accident," I say, almost before I realize I intend to ask about it. There's always been a shroud of mystery surrounding the crash. Probably everyone decided it would be less painful for me not to know the details.

If my parents had been the only ones to die that day, I have no doubt Nox's parents, Gavin and Sylvie, would have taken me in. They would have raised me as their own child, as a sibling to Nox.

But as I'd lost all of them, and Pappa was the highest ranking Council member and next in line to the throne, he was the one to raise me. And the one to give me the news.

He shared only the bare minimum at the time—*terrible accident. All dead. Loved you very much, you'll always have their memories. Now you're leaving this place and moving to Atlanta with me.*

"What do you want to know?" His tone is wary.

But he shouldn't be. I'm not that fragile pre-teen anymore. I'm nearly eighteen now. And if I'm old enough to marry, surely I'm old enough to know the details of the event that took my family from me. He doesn't have to be so close-mouthed about it anymore.

"Just... how it happened. How you learned of it. If they... if they survived for any amount of time afterward or—"

"It was instantaneous," he interrupts. "They didn't suffer. We think there was probably some sort of explosion in the air, shortly after takeoff. Perhaps a bird got into one of the engines and caused a fire."

"I thought it was engine failure."

"Yes, well, it might have been—it wasn't determined conclusively—as far as I know. I was grieving, too, you see. I had little patience for the details at the time, and since then, I've been so focused on you and my job." He pats my hand, and his fingers feel cold. "It's best to just leave it in the past."

"Why wasn't I with them?" Something I've always wondered about, sometimes even wished for. Wouldn't it have been better to die and go to Alfheim with my family than stay here and live without them? Certainly it would have been *easier*. "You said Nox was with them. Why not me?"

"I'm not sure. Who can say? Actually, I thought you *were* with them until later on, when the parents of the girl you were spending the weekend with contacted my office, wondering what was to be done with you."

"Oh." That's a new detail. I always imagined Pappa immediately seeking me out when it happened, rushing to comfort the tragic orphaned girl. But the way he said it just now sounded more like I was a loose thread he'd found sticking out of an expensive scarf *after* getting it home from the store and cutting off the tags.

"Of course then I rushed over and picked you up," he adds hastily. "And you know the rest."

He begins to stand, but still hungry for details, I press further. "It must have been hard for you to become an instant parent to a hormonal tween girl, not to mention one going through post-traumatic stress."

He relaxes again. "I've always said it was my honor to bring you into my home. You know I never married and can't have children of my own, so…"

"Why not?" Another thing I've never dared to ask but always wondered about. I know not all Elven couples can have children. Those who do are usually able to have only one—on rare occasions, two. But if he never married and never… well, how would he know he couldn't…

Rising from the bed and once again wearing the detached expression that's his usual demeanor, he answers, "That's a personal matter. All you need to know is that *you* are my daughter. And my daughter needs to get some sleep. She's got an early flight—and an exciting week ahead."

"Yes Pappa," I say, reading his *conversation's over* tone and sliding off the bed myself toward the bathroom adjoining my room. "See you in the morning."

I turn on the water, and as it warms, I allow myself a tiny bit of anticipation for the week ahead. In less than twenty-four hours I'll be back in the city of my birth, the place I lived with my family and childhood friends. Maybe I'll run into some people who knew them, people who can tell me more stories about them.

My spirit lifts like the steam beginning to fill the room. I might even be able to find out more about their accident and gain a greater sense of closure about it all.

As I step into the shower, another exciting possibility hits me. One of the art schools Mrs. White recommended is in Los Angeles. I tip my head back into the hot stream and smile.

I'll take this trip and do what Pappa wants me to do. But while there, I *might* just do a little of what *I* want as well.

Chapter Seven
Roommate

"I feel like we're in a movie," I tell Ava as our car passes the iconic Hollywood sign sprawled across a distant hill. "It seems like so long ago that I lived here, it's hard to remember that was my life and not just something I dreamed."

Rolling down the window, I let in the warm, but somehow still crisp, air. So different from Georgia in every way. It feels right.

"Welcome back, California Girl," she says, her plump lips stretching over a wide, toothy grin.

Following Ava's instructions, our driver turns up the radio volume. Maroon Five's high happy melody fits the vibe of the day perfectly. Now that I'm here, I'm even more hopeful about the trip. Being away from Pappa's ever watchful presence has me feeling giddy and free, like a kid let loose at Six Flags for the day with a pocketful of money and no parental supervision.

Ava has turned out to be a great travel companion. Only two years older than me, she's far more experienced and navigated the huge Hartsfield International Airport with ease. Same story at LAX. She knows her way around the city as well, having worked and lived here since she was seventeen. The flight passed quickly as she filled me in on her modeling career and life in L.A.

I turn away from the sun-drenched scenery to glance at her. "I can't believe you have your own house."

"Well, I have roommates—I'd be too lonely living in that huge place alone."

The driver takes a left and we begin our ascent into the Hollywood Hills, finally coming to a stop in the drive of an expansive multi-level home that follows the contour of the jagged cliff it's built upon.

"Wow—this is amazing." I open the car door and head for the trunk to get my bag, but the driver has already beat me there.

"I'll take care of these," he says, nodding toward Ava, who's already at the home's modern wood and glass front door and waiting for me with a big anticipatory smile.

"Wait till you see the view."

She leads me inside where I wander through the open floor plan with my mouth gaping. Our houses in Atlanta and D.C. are actually bigger, but this place is way cooler. It's decorated in a sort of retro-seventies style with modern touches. All the furnishings are white, and it seems the entire place is illuminated with light from the floor-to-ceiling window wall, the California sunshine dancing around the room like a Beach Boys song.

I cross over to the window, taking in the view of the valley stretched out below us. "Okay, now I *really* feel like I'm in a movie." My childhood home in L.A. was large but homey, with a swing set in the back yard, and a treehouse, and colorful letter magnets on the refrigerator door. *This* place is unreal.

"We can visit a set while we're here—if you're interested. My roommate Serena is filming this week. She totally wouldn't mind if you want to go watch," Ava says.

"Really? I'd love to. You think we'll have time? My dad made it sound like I'll be booked every minute with the whole agent and photographer thing."

Ava gives me a knowing eyebrow lift. "Your dad isn't here. You *are* pretty tightly scheduled, but there's always time for fun. You just have to know how to work things." She skips off to the kitchen and throws open the door of a huge sub-zero refrigerator. "Want anything? I'm famished."

"Sure. Whatever you have is fine." Unlike what I've read about human models and their starvation diets, Elven girls eat often and eat well. We have much faster metabolisms than humans, and we're tall. Our bodies are naturally thin and athletic—no wonder so many fashion shows and magazines are dominated by our race.

Sometimes I've wondered why the designers and photographers don't get tired of working with the same body type day after day, year after year. Maybe they think it's a good thing, since they basically see models as little more than human clothes hangers or blank canvases for their art.

Speaking of art, I'm dying to get on a computer here and look up the location of the art school in Santa Monica. Pappa uses a parental "spy" software program to monitor my laptop, tablet, and phone, so I'm reluctant to type in the potentially damning words using any of them.

But he doesn't have the same sort of access to Ava's computers, does he? I can't stop a grin from stretching my cheeks. I could get used to this freedom thing.

Eying her backpack, I glance over at Ava, who's setting out pita chips and hummus as well as some fruit. "Mind if I use your laptop to look up some L.A. touristy stuff? I know it's cheesy, but I do want to see some things as long as I'm here."

"Go for it. It's not locked. But Alfred will give you a driver to take you anywhere you want to go, probably, so you don't need to print out directions or anything."

Alfred. Right. My father's friend and the super-agent behind the stellar careers of the world's top actors, musicians, models, and athletes. I read an article about his astonishing rise to prominence thirty years ago, seemingly out of nowhere. What the human writer of that article *didn't* know is the story behind the story—that almost all of Alfred Frey's clients are Elven and that glamour plays a huge part in their celebrity.

I'll be meeting him first thing Monday morning, to launch my own career, I guess. The whole idea still seems very foreign to me. I can much more easily imagine myself behind the camera than in front of it. I love capturing beauty, expressing it with a paintbrush. I can't picture myself as the subject of someone else's art.

And I'm not sure how this whole modeling career thing is supposed to work if Pappa is so determined to marry me off in a political bargain a few months from now—to a reclusive Light Elf.

Ava plops onto the white leather couch beside me, where I've opened her laptop and clicked onto a search engine. She's holding a bowl of the biggest strawberries I've ever seen in my life. As if she's read my mind, she says, "So I heard you're getting married. That's cool."

I glance over at her to see if she's being sarcastic, but there's no indication of it on her face. She seems sincere.

"Yeah, I guess so. Who told you?"

"My mom. She says it's all important and whatnot 'for the people.'"

Her dead-on imitation of her mother's hoity-toity regal tone cracks me up. "Right. That's what my dad says. What about you?"

"Yeah, I know. I'm *old*." She grimaces. At nineteen, she should've been married for a year now already. "But my mom wants me to wait a little longer until I get my career more established and get a good fan pod going. I guess the humans aren't as interested if you're already 'off the market' or whatever."

I hesitate before speaking again. I don't know Ava well. We've seen each other many times over the years, but we've never spent much time talking. I don't know how much I can trust her, how much she buys into her mom's ideas and the mission of the Council. But she seems to be an awful lot like me—very much integrated into the human world, and someone who enjoys her freedom.

"I've been wondering about that—for myself. You know, like, how I'm supposed to marry this guy and have a modeling career? He lives in Altum. Rural Mississippi isn't exactly a fashion mecca. Is he going to move out here so I can work after we're married, or what? And he's a Light Elf, which is weird."

She shrugs and pops a berry into her mouth, speaking between chews. "Who knows what the parentals are thinking? I try to steer clear of all their schemes for *world domination* and just live my life. Maybe he will, though. Maybe he's going to cross over to the *Dark side* and have some kind of performing career and a fan pod as well." She grins at her joke. "Is he a musician or anything? What do you know about him?"

"Nothing," I say on a heavy sigh. "Pappa won't tell me anything and says it's not for me to know about right now—that he's an 'excellent match' and I shouldn't worry about it."

"Wow. You *are* a good girl, aren't you? Mother's always saying, 'Why can't you be more like Vancia Hart? She always does what she's told.'" Ava laughs. "You're making me look bad, girl."

Heat fills my cheeks, though her jibe is good-natured. It's just that I'm embarrassed by how *true* it is. I *do* always do as I'm told. And her teasing reminds me of Carter's comment in the art room yesterday after school, about how it's my life and that maybe I should start making some of my own decisions.

Ava rises from the couch. "Well, I'm going to lay out by the pool. Come on out when you're done. You can bring your food with you if you want to. There's saol water and stuff in the fridge, too."

"Great, thanks." I turn my attention back to my computer search with renewed interest. Finding the website for the art school, I do write down the address, in spite of what Ava said. I won't be asking for a ride from any driver assigned by Alfred Frey—might as well call Pappa and tell him what I'm up to.

No, I'll find my own way to the school. And maybe in some other areas of life as well.

Chapter Eight
The Agent

Alfred Frey's office occupies an entire floor of a Century City high rise. I guess I should have expected no less from a legendary Hollywood agent.

I'm escorted to his door and cross what feels like miles of marble flooring before reaching his desk. He doesn't even look up before muttering, "Sit down."

When he finishes doing… whatever he's doing… he finally lifts his head, moves his eyes over my face and hair, and grunts, "Yes. Yes, it'll work," then drops his gaze back to his paperwork.

Though clearly not human, Alfred doesn't look exactly like the Elves I've seen all my life. He is shorter, less attractive, and yet his face is so interesting it holds its own brand of appeal. If he's really been a top agent for the past thirty years, then the Hollywood crowd undoubtedly assumes he's keeping a plastic surgeon on standby for regular touchups—like all of the Fae, he has an ageless quality about him.

He wears a well-cut suit that has an expensive-looking sheen, a large shiny watch, and several rings. A beautiful turquoise tie matches his eyes and contrasts well with his thick, black hair and deep California tan.

Uncomfortable with the silence, I try to make conversation. "It's nice to meet you. I've heard a lot about you from my fa—"

"Your father wants this done as quickly as possible," he interrupts in a no-nonsense tone. "From what I understand we have no time to waste in getting you launched. I've got you booked on go-sees every day this week, but first you'll need a portfolio. It won't be easy to whip one up so quickly. You'll be working with Stephen Dutton all day—perhaps into the night to get it done."

"All day?" I repeat dumbly.

My online research last night revealed the art school isn't too far from the address of the photography studio listed on the itinerary I was given. I'm hoping to finish the shoot in time to walk the few blocks to the school and check it out before my driver comes back to pick me up.

It might be my only chance to visit the school in person this week. My go-sees could be in different counties or even the other side of the city for all I know—Los Angeles is huge.

"Yes—all day." Alfred's tone is withering. "You're not here for a vacation. We *all* have to do our part—even *Davis Hart's* daughter." The way he worded it and the disgust in his voice makes me wonder—*is* this guy my father's friend? He doesn't sound all that "friendly."

Chastened, I nod and mumble my thanks then follow the secretary who's come to escort me out. I let out a long, shuddering breath as I leave his office. Whatever Alfred Frey is, he is not an ally.

* * *

The Santa Monica studio is cold, with immensely high ceilings and vents that seem to blow from every direction. Shivering in the bikini I was instructed to put on, I try not to wobble too much in my towering heels or squint in the overly bright lights.

"You'll warm up in a minute," the photographer, Stephen, informs me with a deep chuckle that says he's hosted many a shivering girl in this studio. "We have to keep the temperature down in here because of the equipment, but the lights will have you sweating like you're in a sauna pretty soon. So, Alfred says it's your first time in front of a camera, huh?"

I nod, forcing a small smile in his direction, though I can't really see his face with the glare in my eyes.

"You'll do great, don't worry. Alfred knows what he's doing. He's never steered me wrong yet."

I shudder again, but not necessarily from the cold. Alfred sort of creeped me out. He wasn't a lech or anything—he's got a fan pod full of sweet young things if teenaged girls are what he's into. No, it wasn't the way he looked at me, but the way he *didn't*. Though we'd only just met, I got the distinct impression he didn't like me.

Stephen's voice pulls me back to the moment. "Hey,

Sofie, can you powder her again? Thanks."

The photographer was right. I am warming up, and apparently, getting shiny as a result. A small Latina woman steps forward and dusts my face with sneeze-inducing translucent powder, adding another layer to the already thick-feeling makeup on my skin. One *more* new thing to get used to.

"All right. Give me some movement." Stephen gets behind the camera and starts clicking.

Suddenly *movement* seems completely beyond my physical capabilities. I have no idea what to do. I feel stiff and super uncomfortable, like my arms and legs aren't actually parts of my body anymore, but these strange unwieldy things hanging from my joints. I shift from side to side, tilt my head in different directions, but I can sense the disappointment in the room.

In my peripheral vision, the makeup artist and hairstylist lean their heads together and whisper. I'm sure they're talking about how terrible I am. To make up for my lack of "moves," I smile wider and wider until my face aches.

"Maybe vary your expressions for me, Vancia? We've got plenty of smiling," Stephen says. I can almost hear the grimace in his voice.

"Oh. Sorry." If he wants expressions of mortification and dread, then he's getting a lens full now.

So I try to look serious, or *fierce* like that model show on TV talks about. I should have watched that more often.

Stephen steps to the side away from the camera. "Um… let's take a break everyone." Motioning to me with a finger, he says, "Come here Van."

The nickname reminds me of Carter and triggers a sudden bout of homesickness that surprises me. "Are we done?"

His answering expression is a mixture of pity and if-*only*-we-were longing. "Listen kiddo," he says in a gentle tone. "Let's get out of the studio for a while. We have to do some location shoots anyway, and you'll probably have more fun with those."

My shoulders fall. I knew I'd suck at this. "I'm sorry I'm so terrible. I've never—"

"I know. Don't worry about it. It'll come together. You just need to relax a bit. Ever been to Venice beach?"

His imperfect grin really works with his twinkling brown eyes, and suddenly I do feel a bit more relaxed. "Not since I was a kid."

"Well, grab your cover-up and let's go. I'll even buy you a snow cone when we get to Ocean Front Walk."

"Not a cherry one!" The makeup artist warns as she rushes to pack her case and follow us out the studio door.

CHAPTER NINE
FIELD TRIP

Things go a little better on our location shoots. As we move from the beach to a bricked alley, to a colorful mural wall, a rooftop, and back to the studio, changing outfits, hair, and makeup each time, I gradually relax.

Stephen says we got enough usable shots to make a decent portfolio and that he'll print them tonight and have them ready for my go-sees tomorrow.

"You did it, kiddo." He offers me a quick hug.

"If we got anything good, then *you* did it. Thank you for everything. Sorry again for being such a *challenge*."

"Nah, you're a natural," he says, then laughs, probably because we both know he's lying. "But seriously, you'll get the hang of it, and you're going to have some good luck this week—I can feel it. Just believe in yourself. And don't let the other photographers intimidate you. They're not all as *charming* as I am."

I laugh, too, and hug him again. "How could they be?"

Leaving the studio, I check my phone, eager to follow its navigation app to the art school. *Shoot. It's later than I thought.* The clock in the corner of the screen reads five-thirty. Is the school closed for the day already?

I'm supposed to call my driver and let him know when I'm finished, but I stuff my phone back into my purse instead. As far as he and Alfred know, our photo session could go on for several more hours. This is my best chance to visit the school, and I'm going to take it.

I speed-walk down the sidewalk, enjoying the lingering sun and the sound of seagulls flying overhead. I've ditched the ridiculous heels for my usual flip-flops and my long stride helps me make good time. As I pass one guy on the sidewalk, I hear him mutter, "New Yorkers," under his breath. I guess in his laid back, Southern California mind, everyone in a hurry is from New York.

By the time I reach The Dowrey Center for Arts and Design—a square building with lots of windows—my phone tells me it's five-fifty. And of course the hours of operation etched onto the school's glass front doors are eight am to six pm. *Shoot, shoot, shoot.*

Testing the door handle, I'm relieved it swings open. But as I walk down the central hallway, my heart falls again. The place looks basically deserted. The doors lining the hall are all closed, and through the small windows in the center of each one I can see that the lights are off.

I've missed my chance.

The click of a lock and the jingle of keys draw my

attention to the end of the hall. A man stands on the outside of one of the rooms, shifting the items in his shoulder bag. He looks too old to be a student. Is he a professor?

I'm *so* hoping the answer is yes when I call out to him. "Excuse me. Excuse me, sir?"

He looks up and jumps as if startled. "Can I help you?"

Rushing toward him, I speak quickly, putting as much pleasantness into my voice as I can. "Hi. Yes. Do you work here? I was hoping I could see the school. I'm visiting from Georgia, and I was hoping to take a look around? Maybe get an application?"

"Oh. Well, yes, I teach here—Professor Gould."

He extends his hand, and I shake it. "Vancia Hart."

"Unfortunately, we're closing for the day, as you can see. I'm probably the last one in the building." A tiny notch forms between his brows as he studies my hopeful expression. "An application, you said? What semester are you thinking of applying for? The admissions process for this fall is almost completed."

"I know. I—well I just got up the courage to, you know, um check it out. I know I'm kind of behind."

He gives me an understanding smile, starting to walk. "Well, it's never too late to follow your dreams. There might still be a few openings—if not for the fall semester, then the spring. If you come back in the morning and visit the admissions office, they'll give you the forms and set you up with a tour. You can also apply online."

Actually, I can't apply online. Not with Pappa monitoring my computer usage. Maybe I can borrow Ava's computer again. Or… I *could* just use the Sway, something I've avoided in my everyday interactions with humans back in Georgia. But I don't want to.

When it first kicked in as a preteen, I experimented with it. Using it on my human peers always left me feeling guilty, and seeing their zoned out expressions and hearing the obedient tone of their voices kind of freaked me out.

Hopefully, niceness (and begging) will suffice for this situation. Keeping pace with him, I work to remove the hysteria from my voice.

"I can't come back tomorrow. I probably can't come back this week at all, and I really, really *need* to get the application today."

Now that I'm in the building, I'm surprised at how *attached* I feel already to the school. It seems like a place I could belong. If I can fill out an application this week at Ava's house and mail it from there, Pappa will never know. Until there's a *reason* for him to know—a reason that will never exist if I can't convince this guy to help me.

"Maybe… maybe *you* could show me around?"

He stops, and now he really looks at me. Glancing around at the empty hallway first, he brings his gaze back to me and surveys my appearance, his eyes stopping at my purse before returning to my face.

Nope—not big enough for a weapon, Mister. You're safe.

No doubt he's trying to determine what I'm up to—to see if I'm some sort of a threat or just the clueless prospective freshman I've claimed to be.

"I'm not sure," he says, dragging out the last word. "It

really would be better for you to go through the enrollment office. It's not really appropriate for me to give you a tour alone after hours like this."

Shoot. It's not working. *But it has to.* I'll have to use it. *It's not like it will hurt him.*

Touching his arm to stop him from walking away, I gain and capture eye contact with him. *Don't want to lay it on too heavy—just enough to get his help.* I put my will and the minimal amount of Sway I can manage behind my words.

"Please change your mind and show me around, tell me about the school, and then get me an application from the enrollment office. You'll feel good about doing this, and nothing bad will happen as a result of it."

I hold his gaze in mine for a few seconds to make sure it takes then step back and smile at him like the docile Southern belle I'm supposed to be.

He blinks a few times and shakes his head, returning my smile. "As I was saying, I'm so glad you could make it for a tour today. I don't often give them myself, but I'm happy to show you around, answer your questions, and then I'll get you an application to fill out. I'll even make sure to put it in Mrs. Moser's hands personally, with my *highest* recommendation. Now, this is the pottery studio." Pulling his keys from his pocket, he inserts one into the lock of the nearest door.

I follow him in, working hard to maintain my happy expression. I *should* be happy. I'm getting what I wanted. But I hate the *way* I got it.

He hasn't even seen my art portfolio. It could be full of stick figure drawings and crude finger paintings for all he knows, and he's planning to give me his "highest recommendation." Not only could it turn out to be embarrassing for him, it feels like cheating to me.

I don't want to be accepted into art school because I glamoured some poor guy's brains out. I want to earn it—I want my art to speak for itself. I want him to give me an application, not a free pass.

After touring the classrooms and the gallery and stopping by the office for the forms, I follow Professor Gould to the exit doors.

"Thank you so much for the tour. I hope I haven't made you late for anything." It didn't occur to me until just now that his kid could be having a recital tonight or something.

"No, no, my pleasure. And I wish you the best of luck. Like I said, whatever I can do to help." He raises a finger. "Oh—I'm not sure why it didn't occur to me before—long day I guess. I'll need to see your portfolio before speaking to Mrs. Moser. Let me give you my email address and you can send me a zip file, okay?"

My heart lifts from the soles of my shoes and flies up through the top of my head. "Yes. Yes, of course. I'll send it right away. Can't exactly admit me without it, right?" I'm almost delirious with relief that the school will require proof of my talent before admitting me.

"Right" he agrees, and raises a hand in a goodbye gesture as I turn and practically skip down the sidewalk to the photography studio.

My steps slow as I reach the building and turn the corner to the front walk.

The car is there at the curb and my driver is pacing in front of it, phone to his ear.

Chapter Ten
Watched

"So how does it feel to break the rules for once?" Ava stands in the doorway of the guest room, obviously having overheard the end of my phone call with Pappa.

"Um, it feels like I'm going to be on total lockdown for the rest of spring break."

The driver apparently waited for an hour before calling Alfred to report my unscheduled exploration. The agent, in turn, called my father, who just gave me an earful.

"No more going off on your own. You might think you know about big cities, but Los Angeles is not Atlanta, and you have no idea the trouble you can find there. You've been quite sheltered," he said.

Yeah, whose fault is that? That's what I *wanted* to say. Thankfully, he could only hear my thoughts when I consciously directed them at him. What I actually said was, "Yes, Pappa."

"So, did you sneak off with a *boy*?" Ava says, dragging out the last word and grinning ear to ear like she's waiting to be let in on some great conspiracy.

"No. I took a walk… to a school." I wasn't really planning to tell her that last part, but it popped out anyway. Maybe my excitement over the art school is too big to stay penned up inside me.

"A school?" She wrinkles her nose. "*That's* a letdown. When I sneak away, I make sure it's worth my while. Which means, of course, it's to meet a guy."

We laugh together, and I decide to confide in her a bit more. "It *was* actually worth my while. I loved the school. I just hope I can get in—it's really late to apply."

"Oh." She nods. "So you want to come to college in California?"

"Sort of. It's an art school. But please don't tell anyone. I don't want my dad to know. It doesn't exactly fit into his *plan* for my life."

She matches my eye roll with one of her own. "Tell me about it. My mother's plan involves bonding me with some guy in Florida. But I can't get enough of these California boys. It's Mother's fault really. She shouldn't have sent me out here if she didn't want me to sample the local goods."

"Well, unfortunately, that was probably my first and only 'field trip.' I know they're going to watch me every second now."

"There's always a way," Ava says. "If you need to get away again, just tell me and I'll help."

* * *

A messenger delivers my modeling portfolio from Stephen early the next morning. He is some kind of incredible photographer because the photos aren't half bad. I don't even recognize myself in one of them.

The driver arrives to take me on my go-sees. The first is with a clothing designer who makes funky things in loud patterns that all seem to involve polka-dots. She *looks* like someone who'd design crazy circus clothes—bright pink hair, too much makeup, and glasses with giant frames—polka dot, of course.

She says I look young, which she likes. At her request, I do some impromptu posing, which she doesn't seem to like. "Well, you're very green, but still, you might do for the photo spread. I'll call your agent with my decision."

The next one is for lip gloss. I have to smile and pout for no less than ten people, being passed from one to the next as I work my way up the booking chain. It might not sound that hard, but I'm exhausted afterward. All that energy trying to be *pleasing* to strangers. I'm not sure yet what models get paid, but whatever it is, it can't be worth it.

My final go-see is for a teen fashion magazine. The photographer is one of those Stephen warned me about. "Intimidating" is not an adequate word for this guy. He frowns and fusses, barking orders at me to walk, stop, turn around, look at him, stop looking at him, smile, stop smiling. By the time the appointment is finished, I'm ready to pose for the cover of Nervous Breakdown Journal, and I know I'm not going to get the job.

"Okay—you're hired," he growls, sounding like it tortures him to say it. "Be here at five a.m. Thursday morning with clean hair and no makeup—we'll be doing a sunrise shoot."

"Oh. Okay." I back toward the door, still not quite believing it. "Thanks."

He frowns at me, and I hurry out of the room already dreading Thursday. But I am looking forward to some free time before tonight's scheduled event, a trip to a Sunset Strip nightclub with Ava and her roommates Serena and Brenna. It's an officially sanctioned outing, arranged by our mutual agent Alfred and intended to raise all our profiles on the Hollywood social scene.

When the driver drops me back at home, I go in search of Ava and more specifically, her laptop. Thoughts of my parents and their accident have plagued me constantly since my arrival in California. The look of this neighborhood and even the feel of the air here bring back so many childhood memories. I'm hoping some research will turn up the details I need to fill in the many blanks I have about the events that changed my life so drastically five years ago.

Her laptop is in its usual spot, the center of the white leather sofa in the great room. Opening it, my heartbeat trips with the same kind of adrenaline burst I got when Pappa caught me studying with Carter. He's never expressly forbidden me to research details of the crash, but somehow I know he'd disapprove.

I begin typing in the search box when a tiny red light

catches my eye. It's next to the small circular webcam above the screen. My heart leaps up my throat, crashing into my tonsils. I slam the cover down over the keyboard, which probably wasn't smart, but I'm not doing my best thinking at the moment. Questions are whirling inside my brain.

Why is that on? Does that mean someone was watching me?

Probably. What else could it mean? I've heard webcams can be controlled remotely from another computer. Assuming it's not Ava on the other end of the connection— and I'm sure it's not—then it's someone else—someone who should *not* know what I'm searching for.

And if they can watch remotely through the camera, they might also be able to tell what I'm typing. My heart flips again. *Whoever* it is might know about my search yesterday for the art school's address—*Pappa* might already be onto what I'm thinking.

I pace around the great room, to the kitchen, back across the room to the large picture windows, which now that I'm looking, I notice have no covering at all—no shades, no curtains.

Maybe the webcam thing is some creepy stalker who's figured out how to spy on the models and the actress in their own home. Why does that seem less scary than the thought of our parents watching us? In any case, I'm going to tell Ava about it as soon as she gets here.

As if on cue, the door opens and she comes in, dancing to the pop song blasting from her phone. Spotting me, she breaks into a big smile and comes over, looping her arm through mine and pulling me into a little dance with her on the kitchen tile.

"You ready to go shopping?" she asks loudly over the music.

"For what?"

"What?" She turns down the music.

"Shopping for what?"

"For some hot clothes to wear to the club tonight. Alfred has accounts at a bunch of the shops on Rodeo. He likes for us to look good when we go out, and you probably don't have any club clothes, do you?"

"Definitely not."

"Well come on then, girl. Grab your purse. We only have a few hours."

When I tell Ava about the creepy webcam thing, she just shrugs, keeping her eyes on the road ahead. Her car's what you would expect a model in L.A. to drive—a Porsche Cayenne. Appearance is everything, after all, according to the Dark Elven philosophy.

"I'm not surprised," she says. "Alfred's a very 'hands on' agent. He likes to keep tabs on his girls. Or maybe it was my parents."

"Or mine," I say, shuddering.

There will be no more searching on Ava's laptop or any other computerized device in the Model Mansion. And I certainly can't use them to send my art files to Professor Gould. A flicker of panic unsettles my midsection at the thought of leaving here without applying to the school. But on our way to Rodeo Drive I get an idea.

"We passed a library back there," I tell Ava. "Would you mind circling back and dropping me off? I want to… browse around a bit."

"What about shopping?"

"You can pick something out for me—I don't care what it is—you have good taste, and I think we're about the same size."

She shakes her head sadly, looking at me like I'm a bag lady on the roadside or some poor soul on the news who lost her home in a wildfire. "What is the world coming to when a girl would rather shop for books than clothes?"

I grin at her. "Story of my life."

"Okay then," she says on a baffled sigh, taking a left at the next light and executing a U-turn. "I'll come back and pick you up in a while. Don't leave there, though, okay? I'll get in big trouble if I lose you. I don't want your dad yelling at *me*."

"I promise."

Clutching my purse with the flash drive inside, I get out of the car at the curb and walk up the sidewalk with a quick wave over my shoulder. Ava needn't worry about my leaving the library. Not when it's got everything I need—a public computer I can use to email the art files to the professor, *and* to search for some answers about my parents' deaths— all out of range of the spying eyes of Pappa and Alfred.

The automatic door swings open, and I step through with a smile, breathing in the scents of old paper, air conditioning, and hope. Maybe this place holds the answers to my future… and perhaps my past as well.

CHAPTER ELEVEN
CRUSH

I certainly hope Ava's shopping trip is going better than my detective work. Other than the newspaper articles I've read before, the computer search turns up nothing. No death certificates or burial information, no FAA reports or even local police reports on the crash. Maybe that kind of thing isn't available to the public?

I'm thinking about where else I could access that stuff when it occurs to me that this is the perfect time to email Carter. I've been thinking of him these past few days and wondering how his spring break is going.

I type the email, telling him how I utterly suck at modeling and asking about his week so far. He must be on his computer already because his return email is quick.

"Hi. Good to hear from you. I'm sure you don't suck. That much. Ha ha. Are you having any fun?"

I send one back immediately. **"Not yet. Going out on**

the Sunset Strip tonight, though, so maybe." My fingers hesitate before typing the next words, but then I do it quickly and hit send. "I visited an art school. It's amazing. Trying to get up my courage to send in pics of my art portfolio."

There's a long pause before he replies, and I'm wondering if he stepped away from his laptop, but then it comes.

"You'll need this." He attached a photo of my meadow painting—the one I destroyed in that moment of despair. I forgot he took one with his cell phone in the art room that day. I guess he saved it.

It makes me sad to see the painting again, but I'm also grateful to have the photo. As Mrs. White said, it probably was my best to date, and it really should be in my portfolio, especially since I'm applying to the Dowrey Center late and need every advantage I can get.

"Thank you. I appreciate it—you have no idea how much."

"No problem. Glad I could help. Now—send it to the school before you have a chance to chicken out. See? I do know you. Chat you later, tater. Miss you."

I'm torn between laughing at his hokey sendoff and feeling giddy at his last two words. They probably didn't mean anything, but I realize I do miss him. I'm looking forward to seeing him again when I get home.

Which will only be home for a few more months. Before you move away to get married.

Ugh. I compose an email to the address Professor Gould

gave me then pull the flash drive from my purse and attach the zip file full of artwork plus the picture Carter sent me. Taking his advice, I hit send before I can change my mind. Then I log off the computer and whirl in my chair to get up.

And find Ava standing right behind me.

"Oh my gosh, you scared me. How long have you been there?"

"Your painting is very good," she says, wearing a secret smile. "And you have a boyfriend."

"No. I don't. He's not. He's just a friend."

"Sure, that's what I tell my mom about my boyfriends, too. You ready to go? We've got to get back and start getting ready. It might take you a while to squeeze into the teensy mini-dress I bought you."

"Oh no. You didn't," I moan.

She flashes me a dazzling grin. "Oh yes I did. And it's going to look amazing on you. By the end of tonight, you'll have a fan pod waiting list a mile long."

* * *

The atmosphere at Club Crush fits the name—people are packed in like vacuum-sealed almonds. I follow the other girls, squeezing past chattering, laughing people until we reach the edge of the dance floor where there's a little more breathing room. The air smells like beer and cologne, and colored lights flash and change all around us, making the faces appear and disappear in sync with a driving house music beat.

"That's DJ Quattro," Ava's roommate Serena informs me as she pulls me with her to the bar. Flipping her long blonde curls over one shoulder, she lifts a finger to catch the bartender's eye and signal for a drink. "It's house music tonight, but they have rock bands, pop stars in here on different nights. We come a lot—especially when our friends are playing."

"You *know* this guy?" I motion to the famous DJ. Even living way across the country in Atlanta, I know his name. His mixes play on one of our radio stations on Saturday nights.

She leans in close to my ear, though there's no chance of anyone else hearing her over the pounding music. "He's one of us."

"Oh." Now that I really look at him, blocking out the distractions of the lights and the writhing bodies all around us, I can see it. Tall, muscular, carved cheekbones and chin. "What about the bands—are they Fae?" I whisper.

"Some of them are. Some aren't. I'm ready to dance. You?"

She grabs our drinks from the bar top—without paying—and hands one to me, then pulls her other roommate, Brenna with her toward the dance floor. Ava and I follow them out to the center.

Trying to fit in, a take a swallow of the strong drink and move to the music. I like to dance. I'm not that great, but the other girls are—in fact, I'd say Brenna's glamour has something to do with dancing—the way she moves her body is mesmerizing, even to me. It's obvious my companions are entirely at home in this scene, and they're taking their jobs of attracting attention and human admiration seriously.

Serena's already famous. She's had small roles in movies and even a starring one on a TV show. If tonight's anything to judge by, Ava and Brenna aren't too far behind her. Club-goers, male and female alike, stare at them as they laugh and twirl under the lights, drinking their cocktails and generally looking like an ad for Hollywood nightlife.

Of course, the guys stare at them in a *different* way. Which makes me wonder. My temporary roomies know the rules as well as I do. If one of them were to sleep with one of these admirers, that would be it for her—she'd be bonded to him for life and couldn't take another partner.

So what exactly do they do with all that male attention they're courting? No matter how much guys might worship them or try to persuade them, the Elven girls can't actually *do* anything with the human men. Not much anyway. Right? I'll have to ask Ava about it later when we're alone. She's been at this much longer than I have, so she probably knows about that stuff.

Following Alfred's instruction, we've each brought signed headshots in our purses. So embarrassing. But the other girls say that's what we're supposed to do here— get people staring and talking, then give them the cards with our photos on one side and our agent's contact info on the other. Something to do with fan pod recruitment, I guess.

After dancing a while, I'm getting hot and thirsty and I need to go to the bathroom. I tap the closest girl, Brenna, on the shoulder. She spins around and wiggles her slim hips to the music, taking my hands and twirling under one of my arms.

"I'm going to find the bathroom," I half-shout to be heard over the amplified beat.

"I'll go with you," she says and turns toward the other side of the dance floor.

I follow her to a hallway behind the bar. The music's not as loud here, and the lighting's somewhat normal. There's a line for the bathroom, of course. We take our places at the end and study the promotional posters tacked up and down the opposite wall to pass the time.

"Have you seen any of these bands?" I ask her.

She nods vigorously, her bobbed black curls swinging with the motion. "Oh yeah. Practically all of them. I've been out here for three years now, and we go out probably five, six nights a week."

"You go out almost *every* night? How do you get up and do modeling jobs in the morning?"

"Saol water helps a lot." She laughs, pulling a metal flask from her purse and taking a swig. "Want some?"

"Oh, no. I have my own. Thanks."

That makes sense. Saol water is a staple of the Fae diet because of its unique healing and nutritional properties. It's made from a combination of deep root sap and pure underground cavern water distilled over hot mineral rocks.

The only time I've ever seen it made was when I visited Altum as a child during the Assemblage. Manufacturing saol water is more of a Light Elven thing, I guess. I've never heard of Dark Elves making it—we usually live in cities among humans.

"When you move out here for good, you'll probably go out with us a lot," Brenna says. "Maybe even move in with us, since Serena's getting her own house soon. Her fan pod's grown enough that Alfred's ready to set her up with a mansion and pod quarters."

I'm about to ask more about that when one of the posters catches my eye. It's black and red with the words "The Hidden" printed at the top—the band's name I assume. In the center is a black and white photo of the guys in the band. They're all good-looking, clad in the jeans-and-old-t-shirt uniform rock musicians so commonly wear.

The tallest one, standing in the middle and holding a guitar, is the most striking. Dark hair, light eyes, wide shoulders, and a wicked half-grin. I step closer, squinting to get a better view.

My heart rolls over an extra thump, and then it's pounding out a rhythm even the DJ can't keep up with. I fall back several steps until my back meets the wall behind us. My legs are as unstable as overcooked asparagus, and my hands are shaking.

"What's the matter? You okay? You should really have some of this." Brenna offers me her flask again, but I wave it away, never breaking my visual lock on the poster.

"Who… who is that?" I manage to gasp.

"Who?" She turns her head in search of the thing that's grabbed my attention. "Oh—The Hidden? Yeah—they're awesome."

"No. The guy. The guy in the middle."

"Ooohhhh." She drags the word out with a knowing smile. "That's Nox. He's the lead singer and guitar player. You've got good taste. Alfred says he's going to be a huge star."

"Nox," I whisper.

"Hey, the line's moving." Brenna gives me a nudge.

My body responds, and my feet move, but my mind is in another place, another time… five years ago. *Nox Jerrik.* Could it really be him? Could he somehow be alive and playing music clubs on the Sunset Strip?

Nox isn't an uncommon name among our people—his resemblance to my childhood friend is no doubt a coincidence. But the likeness is uncanny. The guy in the poster looks so much like my Nox. Except older. And hotter. And—

I step out of line and snatch the poster off the wall, folding it and stuffing it into my purse.

"What are you doing?" Brenna asks with a chuckle.

I shrug. "I don't know. I… want it."

She nods. "Yeah—pretty much everybody wants a piece of Nox Knight."

Standing up straight, I turn to her. "Knight? That's his last name?"

"Yeah, Nox Knight. Has a good rocker ring to it, doesn't it? Of course, his name could be SpongeBob, and girls would still be dropping their panties every time he gets up on stage and sings." Brenna laughs.

I shudder and step forward in line, the image not sitting well with me, no matter how accurate it might or might not be. I don't like the idea of girls drooling over my childhood sweetheart. But of course, The Hidden's lead singer isn't *my* Nox. He can't be. My Nox is gone.

Most likely *this* guy's a total jerkwad who does enjoy using his glamour to incite panty-dropping. Nox is probably only his stage name, anyway.

And then a thought hits me that makes me stagger and has my heart pounding double time. Maybe *Knight* is a stage name and the guy in the poster *is* actually my old friend, my first puppy love, Nox Jerrik. One thing is for sure—I'm going to find out, and nothing's going to stop me.

Chapter Twelve
Drop-in

By the next afternoon, I feel like I'm going to die if I don't get back to the library. I want to check my email and see if Professor Gould responded, to find out whether he'll help push my application through. And more importantly, I want to search for every bit of information the web has to offer on Nox Knight.

Unfortunately, my whole day is hijacked by a call-back from the lip gloss people. Modeling's still not my favorite thing, but I did my best. I've decided to try harder on *all* my go-sees. If I'm going to defy Pappa and go to art school, I'll have to pay for my own tuition and living expenses somehow. And if smiling and pouting at a camera with extra glossy lips is what it takes, then so be it.

Carter was right—there's no reason I can't do both. If I want to gain my independence and start making my own decisions, then I'll have to become financially independent somehow.

When I finally finish, I fall into the back seat of the car, which is *waiting* for me just outside the shoot location when I emerge—poor driver probably had to sit here all day to make sure I didn't escape again.

"Excuse me," I say to him, leaning forward. "Could we stop by Mr. Frey's office? I need to sign some contracts."

Alfred texted to say he'd messenger the contracts over, but it occurred to me during the shoot today that some face time with him wouldn't be a bad thing for my plan. I can show him how enthusiastic I am about working, tell him how "great" things are going so far... and *maybe* even get some information about Nox Knight while I'm there.

Brenna did say he was a client of Alfred's. It wouldn't be too weird to ask my agent about a fellow client, would it? Only one way to find out. None of the girls know where The Hidden's lead singer lives in Los Angeles—I asked— and I have only a few days left here before returning to Georgia. And only a few *months* left until I'm a married woman—gag.

If my childhood friend really *is* alive and well and in the same city, I'll never forgive myself for not taking advantage of this opportunity to find him while I'm this close. Imagining a tearful, happy reunion with him fuels me as I climb out of the car and head into the gleaming office building.

But as I approach Alfred's office, my steps slow and my bravery falters. Mr. Frey probably doesn't take kindly to unexpected drop-ins. No doubt his schedule is crazy busy. He might not even be in.

Gathering my courage, I force myself to take the last few steps to his receptionist's desk. "Um, hi. I'm Vancia Hart. Remember me from the other day? I was wondering if Mr. Frey would have a few minutes to see me."

"You have no appointment?" Her tone is icy, a thin brow lifting in disdain. After barely glancing at the daily calendar in front of her, she frowns up at me. "I see no appointment for Vancia Hart here." Her name plate reads Rowena—a witch name—figures.

"No. I need to ask him a question about the contracts I'm supposed to sign. It'll only take a few minutes."

No response. This vicious guard dog isn't going to let me get close to Alfred today. She's already beginning the Head Shake of Denial when her desk phone buzzes. Lifting it to her ear, she says nothing, just listens. She nods.

"Yes sir." Then she drops the receiver back into its cradle. "You can go in." She tilts her head toward the massive double wooden doors leading to Alfred's office.

Okaaayy… that's weird. "Thank you."

I push the doors open, and Alfred stands and walks around to the front of his desk.

"Vancia. This is a surprise. What can I do for you?"

His friendly demeanor catches me off guard and nearly makes me forget what I wanted to say. "Oh, I wanted to thank you in person for the help in booking the jobs. It's going great so far, and I think I'm really going to like the work."

His expression falls, almost as if he's disappointed at my enthusiasm. The exact opposite of what I was expecting.

"I see," he says, then smirks. "I'd thought for a moment perhaps you were going to tell me you'd changed your mind and that modeling wasn't for you. I suppose I should have known you'd never go against your *father*'s bidding…"

His tone of voice leaves something hanging in the air between us. An invitation to contradict him? I don't know—it's weird.

"Um… not this time, I guess." Lame and non-committal, but I'm not sure what he's expecting from me. The whole vibe of this meeting is unsettling, from the way he greeted me as if he was actually glad to see me, to his cryptic comment about potentially disobeying Pappa.

Of course, that's *exactly* what I'm planning to do and the only reason I'm here pretending to be eager for a modeling career. I need the money to pay for art school. I'm certainly not going to share that tidbit with Alfred, though. He's probably just spying for Pappa in the wake of my "sneaking off" episode.

Taking a seat in one of the two guest chairs that face his desk, he waves his hand at the other, indicating I should sit as well.

In a soft voice, he says, "I knew your parents—did you know that?"

I drop into the chair opposite him, suddenly breathless. "No. I didn't. Were you their agent?"

"Yes, actually, but we had much more than a professional relationship. We were good friends. I loved both your parents—their deaths destroyed me… as I'm sure, they did you."

I nod in agreement, unable to speak around the huge lump that's formed in my throat.

Alfred's gaze turns to the wide window overlooking Century City. "I remember when you were born. Your father couldn't have been happier if he'd won a Grammy and an Oscar in the same year." Now his gaze is back on me, anchoring me in my chair with its intensity. "They loved you very much, Vancia. Your parents were good people. I miss them."

My response is a whisper. "Thank you. So do I."

"If there's ever a time you'd like to… discuss them…" He stands abruptly and walks around to the other side of his desk. "Well, I suppose you'd better be on your way. I have an appointment in two minutes. Here are your contracts." He shoves some documents at me. "You may sign them and leave them with Rowena or take them with you and look them over first. You know how to reach me."

Thoroughly baffled by our exchange and its sudden end, I take the papers and walk toward the door, turning his words over in my mind as I cross the expanse of carpet. Just as I reach the door, I have a fresh burst of daring. *It's now or never.*

I spin back to face Alfred. "You represent Nox Knight and The Hidden, right?"

He looks up from his desktop. "Yes. Why do you ask?"

"No reason, really. When I was out with Ava and the girls last night, I saw their poster in the club. Nox looked familiar to me."

Alfred's eyes narrow, making them gleam even from

across the room. "Yes, he reminds me of someone, too—another old friend of mine—very musical as well. Unfortunately, he's no longer with us. I've lost too many friends." After a pause, he adds, "One would *think* Nox comes from a very long line of musical glamour, but when I asked about his family, I didn't recognize the names he gave me. Not that I would, I suppose. He hails from Mississippi—has recently graduated high school there."

"Mississippi? Really? That's… interesting."

Everyone in the Fae world knows Mississippi is the territory of the Light Elves, and the seat of their political and royal power, Altum. But Nox Knight couldn't be a Light Elf—they don't mix with humans, much less perform in front of them.

"It is, isn't it?" Alfred says.

"So then, I guess he doesn't live in Los Angeles." I can't keep the disappointment out of my voice entirely.

"Oh, no. He does have a home here—in Malibu right on the beach, in fact. Have you seen Malibu?" Alfred lifts a brow in an expression that seems significant somehow. "The area just west of Zuma along Broad Beach Road is so lovely. I'm especially fond of the Spanish tiled roofs some of the homes have there. You should make a point of visiting the area before you leave town. You might find it… an enlightening sight."

Is he telling me where Nox's house is?

It seems that way. Either that or he's suddenly feeling chatty and dispensing tourism advice. But why would he tell me where to find Nox? Unless… unless he wants me to

79

see him and help determine his identity, to confirm or dispel his own suspicions.

Even *if* that's what's going on, and a bigger "if"—if Nox Knight and Nox Jerrik are one and the same—I'm not sure I'd share my discovery with Alfred Frey. My whole life I've heard of him as a friend of Pappa's, and this change of demeanor is a little too much for me to swallow.

And if Nox *is* alive—and didn't die in that plane crash with his parents—I'm not sure Pappa is a friend of *his*.

Chapter Thirteen
Malibu

I ask the driver to take me to Malibu to "see the sights" before driving me back to Ava's house. It's nearly sunset, and as Alfred said, the area's beautiful. And just as he said, there's a string of lovely—and huge—beach homes along Broad Beach road near Zuma. The neighborhood's certainly fit for a rock star.

"Could you stop here please? I'd like to walk for a while," I tell the driver. Asking him to wait, I get out and stroll down the street until I find a point of beach access. I don't want him to see me knocking on doors on the street side.

After pushing through a particularly sticky access gate covered in private property signs, I walk along the high tide line, checking out the back sides of the exclusive mansions. The beach itself is lovely, and nearly deserted. The Pacific water feels cold on my toes, contrasting with the warm breeze, but I'm not here for a beach day—I'm here to stalk a celebrity. And I have no idea what I'm doing.

This is idiotic. How am I supposed to tell which house is his?

And then I spot the red Spanish tile roof. The style of the home is different from the modernistic wood and glass structures surrounding it. Is this what Alfred was getting at when he mentioned the style of home he "admires?"

Heart pounding and half-expecting a beefy bodyguard to challenge me, I approach the house and climb its back stairs. The chime of the doorbell sounds like an electric guitar chord. That has to be a good sign, right?

I think no one's going to answer when, finally, a small woman in a crisp blue uniform opens the door and asks in heavily accented English, "I help you?"

I put on my most innocent smile. "Yes. I'm a friend of Nox's. I was out for a walk and thought I'd stop in to say hi. Is he home?"

"No. No Mr. Nox here," she says as she starts to push the door closed, her eyes wide with alarm.

My hand stops her from succeeding. Though she claims he doesn't live here, the fact that she called him "Mr. Nox" lets me know I have the right house.

"Oh, well, when will he be back?" I ask in a cheery voice, refusing to be dissuaded. Again, I could just Sway her, but I'd rather not.

"No," she repeats, sounding a bit more frantic this time. I'm thinking maybe his staff is forbidden to answer the door and this lady broke the rules. She's obviously panicking now and trying harder to shut the door on me.

Well, I tried. Besides, she'll feel better about her "mistake" if she doesn't even remember it, right?

Focusing my eyes on hers, I will her to answer me. "What's your name?"

"Marta," she answers in a dazed way.

"Marta, please tell me where Mr. Nox is. *Is* he home?"

"No. Mr. Nox leave for Mississippi this morning. He comes back three months."

Shoot. Three months is far too late for me. I'll be back home in Atlanta by then and preparing for my wedding. I can't believe I've gotten so close, yet I'm still so far from finding out if this guitar-playing, panty-influencing Nox is in reality my beloved childhood friend.

"Thank you, Marta. You can return to your work. And you will not remember meeting me or having this conversation."

"Okay," she answers woodenly, which makes me feel bad all over again. I'd hate to see the human brain on glamour. A CAT scan would probably resemble a person on some sort of mind-bending drugs.

Walking back down the beach toward where I left the car, I try to figure out what comes next. After graduation next month I'm sure Pappa will expect me to fly back out here and get down to work on my modeling career. And then in June, it's off to Altum and my "destiny" as a royal bride. Unless I stand up to Pappa before then and tell him I won't go through with it—that I'm enrolling in art school instead.

Just imagining that conversation makes me shiver in the

hot California sun. I have no doubt Pappa's reaction to such a declaration would be… not good. He'd probably lock me up until June and drag me to Altum in handcuffs, if necessary.

I can't risk that. I really want to graduate. I want to see my classmates, to see Carter again. And I can't make any progress toward changing my future if I'm a hostage in my own home.

No, I've got to *keep* my secret plans a secret. I'll have to pretend to go along with Pappa's design for my life and for my impending wedding. But I know now for sure—I can't really go through with it.

Even *if* my new husband—ugh—was to move out to California with me, even *if* he *allowed* me to attend art school in addition to modeling, I have a whole new reason now for not wanting an arranged marriage.

I have to find out the truth about Nox Jerrik *before* becoming someone else's wife. Because if he's still alive… everything changes.

CHAPTER FOURTEEN
HOME AGAIN

We make one more stop on the way back from Malibu. The driver waits at the curb while I run into the library under the guise of needing a new book to read out by the pool.

I log onto a computer and check my email. There's a new one from Carter—a few lines saying he's looking forward to my return, which is nice. And then I see the one I'm hoping for. It's from Professor Gould.

My finger trembles as I tap the key to open it.

> **Dear Ms. Hart,**
> I received your portfolio and application and passed them along to our head of school, Mrs. Moser. I am pleased to inform you that you have been admitted and may be eligible for some scholarship money as well. Please have

your parents fill out the attached financial forms and send them to this address—"

The email goes on, ending with a big congratulations and official welcome to the Dowrey school, but I'm basically skimming at this point.

I got in! I'm going to art school!

I want to jump up and dance in the library but somehow manage to restrain myself. And now I'm dying to see Carter, too. Because he's the only person—aside from Ava—that I can really share my excitement with.

Grabbing the first book I see, I toss it on the counter, take out a new library card first, and then check out the book to support my cover story. I force myself not to skip on the way to the car, but inside I'm celebrating because now I know for sure what my future looks like, and it does not include marriage at eighteen to a stranger.

In a few days I'll be under Pappa's roof—and under his thumb—in Atlanta again. But come fall, I'll be back here and living life on my own terms. I just have to figure out the right time and the best way to inform the leader of the Dark Elves that I'm going to defy him.

* * *

By the time my plane lands in Atlanta, I've almost decided to just go ahead and tell Pappa about the art school and the scholarship. Maybe he'll be proud of me, especially when I tell him that I'll continue modeling as well. Anyway, it's my life, and I'm nearly a legal adult. He can't actually *force* me into this marriage if I outright refuse, right? We may be Elves, but this is America.

He didn't pick me up as I thought he might. Instead, he sent his driver to the airport to get me. Once home, I step through the door and call out, "Pappa?" Surely he didn't go to bed without seeing me first?

"Pappa," I continue to call, walking down the hallway to his home office.

The light is on, shining under the door onto the marble hallway floor. *Must be working late*. I rap on the door lightly then open it and peek in. He's sitting at his desk, talking on the phone, but gestures me in with two fingers.

Silently, I cross the floor and flop into the plush chair facing his desk, offering him a tired smile. We've never spent an entire week apart since the day I came to live with him, and I've actually missed him.

Yes, he's demanding and less than affectionate, but he's still the most constant presence in my life, and he's taken care of all my needs for the past five years. Our relationship might not be like the one I shared with my mom and dad, but he's the only "parent" I've got left.

Hanging up the phone, Pappa asks in a low, calm voice, "How was your trip?"

Something's wrong.

His tone is off. The question feels like a baited trap, and my heart becomes a hummingbird thrashing against a plate glass window.

All thoughts of coming clean flee my brain. This—*this* is why I felt the need to hide my activities in the first place.

There's something about Pappa that's a little frightening, even when he's smiling as he's doing now.

I force a carefree tone I don't feel. "It was great. I think my modeling jobs went well—the clients seemed happy. And I had a good time with Ava. I enjoyed meeting her roommates."

Pappa's smile remains, but his eyes harden into the same predatory scrutiny he usually reserves for humans. "Apparently that's not *all* you enjoyed."

My pulse throbs so hard I'm afraid my eyeballs are bulging in and out in time with its rhythm. "What do you mean?"

One heavy, dark brow lifts. "It looks like you enjoyed your *freedom* as well."

He tosses some papers onto the desktop between us where they land with a smack. Trying to control my quaking hands, I reach for the pages and pull them into my lap, and all the air leaves my lungs at once.

Print-outs of my emails from the library. The two with Carter. The two between myself and Professor Gould. How did he get these? How did he know?

I look up at his face, and I'm sure he can read the terror in mine. But he smiles again. This time there's no mistaking the malevolence in the expression.

"After all I've done for you, Vancia, I must say—this hurts me."

I shake my head. "I didn't want to hurt you. I just want to live my life. How did you…"

Leaning forward across the desk, he drills me into my seat

back with his stare. "As I've told you before, *dear daughter*, we all have a role to play—a job to do for the greater good of our people. Your new friend Ava did her job."

"Ava?" A pang of betrayal squeezes my heart. "*She* told you. Was her job... to *spy* on me?"

"She was instructed to look out for you, and that's exactly what she's done. Don't look so offended." He laughs, relaxing into the high leather back of his desk chair. "It's not as if keeping a watch on you was unnecessary, is it? It's a good thing she was faithful to her task. Your... *dallying* could have ruined everything for all of us."

He stands now, coming around to the front of the desk and towering over my seated position. "There will *be* no art school. And there will be *no* more communication with this human boy. If you care about his... *welfare* at all, you'll obey me in this."

I spring up from my chair to face him. "You leave Carter alone. If anything happens to him—"

Pappa's head drops back and he laughs loudly. "You're threatening me? What will you do? Hmmm? This plan is not only mine, but the High Council's. Do you know how embarrassing it will be for me to face them again after what you've done? By now, Thora has informed them all about your *extracurricular activities*. I never dreamed my own daughter would shame me before my subjects."

Anger burns my gut like ghost pepper sauce. Anger toward Ava for deceiving me. Toward the Council and their schemes. But mostly toward Pappa, for bringing up the idea of hurting my friend. For caring more about what the

Council thinks than about what I might want. And for laughing at my feelings and hopes and dreams.

My voice is a low scrape in the quiet of his luxurious office. "You're not my *real* father. My parents were Calder and Eira. And they're dead."

All amusement slides from Pappa's face. "Yes. They are." He leans in close enough for me to feel his hot breath strike my cheek. "And unless you'd like to join them in Alfheim, you'll do as you're told and remain *useful* to me. Never forget—you're not my *real* daughter, either."

Chapter Fifteen
Sweet Sorrow

"Hey, what's up Tink?" Carter approaches me with a huge grin as I'm shutting my locker Monday afternoon.

"Hi," I wheeze, my nerves short-circuiting at the sight of him. How am I supposed to do this—cut him off, *stop* being friends, or whatever we are?

He gives me a quizzical glance, head tilted to the side, brows raised. "You still jet-lagging?"

No doubt he's wondering why I never returned his last email. Or called.

Even if I dared to do it, I couldn't. Pappa took away my laptop and tablet and phone. I've been living in the Dark Ages for the past few days, and I don't know how long it will last—probably until my *blessed* wedding day. Maybe even after that, when I'll trade a controlling father for a possibly more controlling husband. I'm officially a prisoner in my own life.

"I'm fine," I say without emotion, without looking at him.

"Oookaaay." Carter drags the word out, waiting for some sort of explanation for my pissy mood, I guess. When I fail to offer one, he tries again. "So, you have a good time in L.A.? Am I going to see your lovely face on the front of a magazine at CVS soon?"

"I'm late," I say. "I've got to go. Sorry." Like a complete coward, I whirl away and start toward my next class, trying to leave him behind. I have to—physically and emotionally.

But Carter catches up to me and drops a hand on my shoulder, stopping my forward motion and turning me around to face him. "What's going on, Vancia? Are you okay? Did I do something wrong?"

Sighing and blinking back some really ill-timed tears, I say. "No. You didn't do anything. It's just… I got into the art school."

"Well that's great! So why—"

I shake my head. "I'm not going. Pappa found out and put his foot down."

Now Carter's normally jovial eyes turn stormy. "He can't do that. That's your dream. And it's your life. You've got to do it anyway, Van. There's got to be a way."

"No," I shake my head repeatedly. "There's not."

He frowns. "Well, maybe I can—"

"What?" I snap back. "Maybe you can what? Debate my father and make him change his mind? Give me the money yourself?"

My frustration-fueled jab hits its mark. Carter's hopeful

gaze drops to the streaked linoleum floor between us.

"Well, no. But I was thinking—I could maybe get a job out in California—I've always wanted to see it. We could, I don't know, be roommates or something, and you wouldn't need to rely on your father because…" His voice drifts off into an embarrassed silence.

A tear spills over onto my cheek. I wipe it away with one hand, wrapping the other arm tightly around my ribcage. "Carter… we hardly know each other."

"I know. I know it's stupid—I just want the chance to *get* to know you—I don't want you to go away and never see you again. I feel like there's something between us. Or there could be."

I let out a shaky exhale, at a loss for words. He's stunned me to the core with his proposition—and how much it appeals to me.

"I don't know what to say. I wish… I want…" I can't say what I want. I'm not allowed to want what I want.

Carter moves forward and wraps a hand around the back of my head, pulling my face to his. Before I can even think to protest, our lips come together and he's kissing me. Right here in the hallway at school, like the couples I've seen together over the years—human couples.

The rush of pulsing sound between my ears drowns out the banging of locker doors and hallway conversation. There's only Carter's sweet, hot mouth moving against mine and the soft strikes of his rapid breathing on my cheek. My heart is rolling around inside my chest like it's searching for the emergency exit.

My first kiss—well, except for the one Nox gave me about a week before the plane crash. *Nox.*

I pull away and stare up into Carter's blue eyes, so open, so innocent, so unaware of the dangers my world presents to him. If there was something sinister behind the plane crash—*if* Pappa is so secretive about it for a reason…

"I've wanted to do that for a while now," he says with a pleased grin.

Shaking my head sadly, I step back to put some room between me and the sweet, smiling boy in front of me. The boy I'm endangering just by being here with him. "Carter… you have no idea how much your offer means to me, how much your… friendship means. But moving out to California together would never work. My father is not what he seems. He's more powerful than you can imagine, and he's… dangerous. I can't go against him, and if I did, I certainly wouldn't involve you."

Carter's gaze grabs mine with a ferocity I've never seen in him before. He re-closes the distance between us and takes my hand, squeezing it. "I already *am* involved. And if you're really scared of your dad—there's no way I'm letting you go through this alone."

"No. You're *not* involved. You can never be."

A new sense of comprehension enters his eyes. "I understand. You don't feel the same way about me." He releases my fingers and nods with a hard swallow.

"It's because I do care about you that I have to do this. We can't… we can't study together anymore. Or email. Or anything else."

He continues to nod, but I can tell he doesn't believe me.

"I get it. Well, take care of yourself then. And Tink—" He steps back a couple of paces, preparing to turn in the opposite direction. "You *can* have the life you want. You can do anything you set your mind to. I don't know where you'll end up—but don't *give* up, okay? I'd hate to see that beautiful light go out."

The bell rings as he walks away. I stay in place, watching him go, watching the distance between us grow.

* * *

At dinner that night, Pappa and I eat in silence. Finally, as a servant clears the dishes and he's beginning to rise from his chair, I say something.

"May I speak with you?"

"If you're going to try to argue with me—"

"I'm not."

He sits back down and tents his fingers under his chin, elbows on the table, waiting for me to continue.

"I wanted to say I'm sorry. I realize you're trying to do what's best for everyone—for me. And I apologize for sneaking around behind your back, and for… saying you're not really my father. You've been very good to me, and I'm grateful for all you've done."

He gives me a sincere smile. "Thank you for saying that."

"And…" Here my voice almost fails me. The words that are about to come out of my mouth are so opposite of what's in my heart that it's difficult to force them. "I will do what you ask. I'll drop the idea of art school. I'll do the modeling and have a fan pod when the time's right. And I'll marry the son of Ivar."

The smile turns into a beam of light. It's the happiest I've ever seen Pappa, including at his most recent election-night victory party. "This is wonderful news, Vancia." He tilts his head and narrows his eyes. "Of course, you're still under restriction—temporarily. I cannot let you have your computers and phone back yet."

"That's okay. I understand."

And I don't care. I don't need them—not for the new plan I have in mind.

No, the allies I plan to enlist don't even use email or phones or any other form of modern technology. I'll need to see them in person. And that means going with Pappa to Mississippi.

To Altum.

To the home of the Light Elves.

Chapter Sixteen
Bridal Suite

Dirt. No matter which way I turn, all I see is dirt. *How do they stand it?*

I've been here in the underground Kingdom of Altum for three days now, and I've scarcely been allowed to leave my room. It's nice enough, I suppose.

To be fair, the earthen walls aren't exactly *dirty*—they're more like stucco, tightly packed and textured. But there are no windows, and the glowing mineral rocks that provide room lighting give everything an unreal, mystical quality, like we're living in some ancient fairy tale.

The furniture here is all heavy and made of ornately carved wood. I haven't seen a manmade fiber since we arrived. The Light Elves certainly *look* like the Elves from my tribe, but they act nothing like them, and where I'm so used to communicating through speech, none of them speak out loud. The ones I've interacted with so far have been kind, but all the mind-to-mind communication with these nature-lovers is giving me a headache.

I've yet to meet my groom—bad luck, Pappa says—and I suppose that's why I'm stuck here in our assigned quarters until the ceremony, being served and pampered with pre-wedding beauty treatments and dress-fittings.

Maybe I'd actually enjoy all of it if I weren't so desperate to speak to Ivar, to tell him about my father's *real* motivation for the wedding—using me to control the heir to the Light Throne. Of course, Pappa says it's all about *uniting* our people so we can join forces against the humans and claim rulership over them, to be worshipped and served by them once again as it was in the Old Days. Either way, I want no part of it.

My hope is that once Ivar knows the truth, he'll call the arrangement off, and I'll be free to leave and resume my search for Nox Knight.

According to what Nox's housekeeper said, there's still another week or two before he returns to California. That means he could be here in this very state right now—in this town even. And I'm trapped underground, wasting precious time.

The door to my room opens, and I look up from my book, jumping in guilty surprise.

Pappa strides in. "How's my girl?" His tone is light, cheerful. His meetings today with the other tribes must have gone well.

"I'm fine, Pappa. Just bored. I'm ready to get this thing over with."

"That doesn't sound like an eager bride."

I give him a sweet smile. A good-daughter smile. "You know what I mean. I haven't even been allowed to meet him yet. My nerves are going crazy. What if we hate each other? What if he's mean and ugly?"

Pappa chuckles. "I assure you he's not ugly. I've met the young man. He seems a bit apprehensive as well, but I don't think he's mean."

Hearing that my intended groom might not be all-in either gives me a jolt. It actually makes me like him a little. I guess I haven't considered before now that he, also, might be doing this against his will or out of a sense of duty. Maybe the Light Elves aren't so different after all.

Pappa crosses the room to the bed and runs his fingertips over the wedding dress I left wadded up there when I last pulled it off. He glances back over his shoulder at me, his eyes narrowing.

Are you excited about tomorrow?

He asked the question in the old Elven way. Which makes me nervous. He'll expect me to answer him in similar fashion, which means lying will be impossible. Could he somehow know what I'm planning? No, there's no way. I told no one this time. There *is* no one I can trust. I'm on my own—now and especially later, after I betray Pappa and tell his enemy clan what he's really up to.

Yes, Pappa. It's the most important day of my life. And that's one hundred percent true. Tomorrow is the day I start standing up for myself, start doing what's right for me instead of blindly following Pappa's orders. My own little Independence Day.

He nods and goes to the door, leaving without another word.

I don't like the thought of losing his love. But then, I'm not really sure I ever had it in the first place. *Love* is not something that's high on his list of priorities. He's so filled with hatred for the humans and his desire to dominate them that there's no room in his heart for anything else.

CHAPTER SEVENTEEN
WEDDING DAY

For the first time in my life, I feel like a princess. No less than three attendants are helping me dress, doing my hair, preparing me to marry a prince. It's uncomfortable, and certainly unfamiliar, to be served like this. And if all goes well, it will be completely unnecessary.

Though I was born the daughter of the Dark Elf king, I never saw my parents act like royalty. They certainly didn't raise me to behave as if I were different or somehow better than the other children I knew. But as I turn to observe myself in the full-length mirror, I definitely *look* different.

The white dress is made of Elven hand-spun material, light as a spider web on my skin, achingly beautiful, with a sheen that makes it seem to glow from within.

Whatever they've done to my hair makes its natural platinum color shimmer like moonlight. I've been drinking saol water straight from the source since arriving, and my skin has benefitted, also bearing the healthful, clear glow that is the hallmark of the Light Elves.

If I were a *real* bride and actually planning to go through with this, I'd be delighted with my wedding day look. But as things stand, it feels more like I'm all dressed up for my own funeral.

The life I've known will die today. My relationship with my adoptive father will die. I suppose there's a small chance my actions could lead to my *actual* death. I don't know King Ivar. Will he be so furious about the deception that he'll react with deadly force? Could Pappa ever be angry enough with me to sentence me to death for my insubordination instead of just banishing me?

It doesn't matter. I study my reflection and my jaw sets. My eyes look different now, too. They are filled with a new determination—to change my life and my destiny—or die trying.

The door to my quarters opens, and the woman in charge of ceremony planning steps in. *Are you ready?* she asks.

I am.

I follow her down the hall, my train flowing behind me. Will I get a chance to even meet my groom and his father before the ceremony, or will I have to announce my refusal during the actual event, in front of hundreds of witnesses? I am truly hoping it doesn't have to happen that way. I have no wish to publicly humiliate Pappa.

I just want out. I want my own life.

The murmur of a large crowd steadily grows as we near

the ballroom of the royal residence. We pass the doors, which are slightly ajar, and I get a glimpse inside. My heart flips, then flips back over again.

The space is filled with colored light, fancifully dressed people. This is a bigger event than I'd even pictured. There aren't hundreds of witnesses, but thousands. Wonderful.

Thankfully, the wedding organizer leads me to a small sitting room near the entrance to the ballroom. I still have a few more minutes to gather my courage and make my peace with whatever may come.

Wait here.

She leaves me, and I fall into a chair in one corner, nervously running my fingertips over my freshly buffed and shined nails.

I can do this. I can do this.

I start to picture the reaction of the attending crowd when I stop the ceremony and make my shocking announcement, and then I banish the mental picture. If I think too much about the consequences, I might not go through with it.

And then I'm no longer alone.

Into the small room steps King Ivar. Suddenly, I remember him from the Assemblage ten years ago. He looks the same—all tall, square-jawed handsomeness, with dark golden curls and piercing green eyes. From the way he carries his body to the expression on his face, he epitomizes leadership. This is a king, in every way. Compared to him, Pappa seems… well, he seems *less*.

Following shortly behind him, a young guy comes in.

There's no doubt he's the king's son—he looks exactly like him. For the first time, I'm looking at the boy I've been betrothed to since I was twelve. Only he's not a boy. If this guy were to set foot in my high school back in Atlanta, there would be some sort of hormone-infused girl-fight in the cafeteria.

Like his father, he's tall, broad-shouldered, with loose blond curls and remarkable green eyes. My fiancé is probably the best-looking eighteen year old I've ever seen in my life. And there's no way I can marry him.

I rise to greet them. Instantly a tremor begins in my fingers. The tiny earthquake travels up my arms, to my stomach, down to my legs where it settles in, making me want to fall back into my chair.

I close my eyes and breathe deeply. I can do this.

Greetings Vancia, and welcome to our home. I trust this occasion is as happy for you as it is for... all of us? The king shifts his face slightly to give his son the evil eye, as if daring him to disagree.

This is it. My opportunity to say what I've come to say. *Well, actually...*

The door opens again, and a panicked-looking servant pokes his head in, capturing the full attention of my groom and his father. And then the younger guy spins and runs from the room. Heaving a heavy sigh, King Ivar turns back to me.

Forgive my son. And excuse me for a moment. We have an unexpected visitor and must deal with her. I shall return shortly. He sweeps from the room, leaving me breathless and confused.

Her? Who would dare come to Altum uninvited? I sit, but stand again after only a minute. Pacing the room, I start on my fingernails once more. What's going on? What if they don't come back before the ceremony? I didn't get a chance to tell Ivar about Pappa's plan.

Finally I peer from the room into the empty hallway. Around the corner is the ballroom and past that, the entrance to the royal dwelling. If there's a visitor—that's where she'd be, right?

Looking left then right, scanning the hall, I leave the room and make my way toward the front door. Indeed, my groom is visible through the open doorway. Just beyond him, I see the back of his father's head. Crossing the distance to the door, I stand just inside, watching.

Clearly the king is engaged in a very serious conversation. Since it's all conducted in our native language, I can't hear it. When we communicate silently, our messages go only to the person for whom we intend them, like text messaging, rather than Facebook.

But then I do hear something—a human voice—a girl's voice. And then my fiancé speaks—out loud. I didn't even know he could do that. I can't stand it any longer. I slip through the opening and go to his side, touching his shoulder.

Is everything all right? Who is this?

He tears his eyes from the human girl and gives me his attention. His gaze is wild, desperate-looking. *I'm sorry. I haven't seen her for a while. I don't know what she's doing here. Please go back inside, and I'll explain later.*

Darting one last glance at the pretty, sad-looking girl, I turn and go back to my small sitting room. So *this* is why my fiancé seems so reluctant to follow through with the ceremony. There's someone else. A human. Is the son of the Light Elf king actually in love with her? I can't prevent a hysterical laugh from escaping my lips. I would never have dreamed there'd be a scandal to top the one I'm about to cause.

The pounding of footsteps draws my attention to the open door, and I see the prince's back disappear into the darkness at the far end of the corridor. Another involuntary giggle erupts. Maybe this conversation with King Ivar won't be necessary after all. Apparently I have a runaway groom.

After another few minutes, the king returns. *Forgive the interruption. My son will join us momentarily—he needs a few moments to regain his composure.*

No he doesn't, I say.

Excuse me?

He doesn't need to go through with this. I look straight into Ivar's eyes, hoping he'll be able to read my utter sincerity. *I don't want to marry your son. Nothing against him or you. It's because I don't want to deceive either of you.*

The king's eyes widen, but he doesn't respond, only stares, waiting for me to continue.

My father's intentions for this marriage are not pure. He wants me to influence your son. He wants to use us both to draw your people into his scheme to enslave the humans, to bring back the old order of Elven rule and human subjugation. I look down at my feet, ashamed to have ever considered going along with the plan. *I'm so sorry it's gone this far. I don't want to dishonor my father or your son, but I cannot go through with this.*

There is no answer. Looking back up to see Ivar's reaction, I'm shocked to see his eyes fill with tears. Finally, he responds.

Thank you for telling me this. Of course, I release you from the marriage pact. But you may not be welcome to live among your people after this. Please know you will always have a home among mine.

Thank you. But I plan to go my own way. Hesitating, I finally gather the courage to ask about his puzzling emotional reaction—I'd expected anger, not sorrow. *Are you well, sir?*

He nods. *I'm ashamed of myself—I have a lot of work to do to repair my relationship with my son. I need to go find him. Remember what I said about your father—be careful. From what I know of him, mercy is not his first nature.*

I will.

He leaves the room and strides down the corridor where my now-ex-fiancé disappeared. I emerge from the room and turn in a bewildered circle. Where to go now? What to do?

I'll have to face Pappa eventually, so I might as well find him and get that over with. He's probably glad-handing inside the ballroom, accepting congratulations as the father of the bride-and-future-queen. Oh, this is not going to be a pretty conversation.

Chapter Eighteen
Sighting

I grasp one of the ballroom's double door handles, preparing to seek out Pappa and discreetly lead him to a private location where we can talk. Happy sounds drift through into the hallway—clinking glasses, lilting Fae music, and laughter. The crowd inside is ready for a good time, a celebration.

Taking one last fortifying breath, I press a clenched fist into my stomach to quell the stampede of butterflies gathering steam. I squeeze my eyelids shut and give the handle a tug. But my fingers loosen and the door softly closes again when a voice grabs my attention. A loud voice. An angry voice. It's coming from just outside the royal residence, in the common area.

She's still here.

Unable to resist one last peek at the girl who's claimed the heart of the Elven prince—my former fiancé—I go to the palace's front door and peer through the opening.

She stands in the middle of the path, halfway between my hiding place and the tunnel that leads out of Altum. She's upset. And she's not alone.

Her face is red, her hands clenched, as she argues with an extremely tall, dark-haired Elven guy whose back is to me. Maybe he's a guard who's kicking her out or something?

But no, she's storming away, and he's grabbing her sleeve to stop her. *Interesting.* There's more heated conversation, the words of which I'm too far away to understand, and then she succeeds in pushing him away and runs toward the opening of the tunnel to the surface.

The guy stares after her, tension holding his powerful body in a state of suspended animation. Then his shoulders fall, and he slowly turns my way.

Oh my God.

By the time I see him in profile, my adrenaline is spiking to fight-or-flight levels. Could it really be him? I fling open the doors and launch myself through them.

And my entire body jerks back as if I've been struck by a moving vehicle. Something has snagged my dress, and I'm going down fast, but I don't hit the ground. Powerful arms catch my fall a moment before my head impacts the stone floor.

"What have you done?" Pappa yells, yanking me upright to face him. He slams the door shut, closing out the shadowy male figure in the distance.

Pulling toward the door in desperation, I try to wrench myself away from Pappa. "I… I need to go—I need to see—"

"You're not going *anywhere* until you explain to me why I've just been informed there will be no wedding today."

His grip on my bare upper arms is punishing, fingertips digging into the tender flesh. Squirming in an attempt to dislodge them only makes his hold tighter.

"I can't do it Pappa," I cry. "It's wrong. You've always warned me that bonding is forever. I can't bond myself to someone based on a lie. Especially when he's as opposed to it as I am."

The veins in Pappa's neck bulge dangerously. "You talked to him. You *told* him."

"I told the king. I didn't get a chance to tell his son. It's for the best, Pappa. You'll see."

I hear the crack of his palm striking my cheek a split second before the stinging pain registers in my brain. Staggering backward, I stare at Pappa in shock.

"The only thing I see," he hisses, his pointing finger shaking in the air between us. "Is a foolish girl who's destroyed five years of my careful work in one moment of ignorant self-interest. You have *no idea* what you've done. You will regret this."

Holding my fingers to my throbbing cheek, I respond in a voice thick with tears. "I regret disappointing you. But you're wrong. I do know what I've done—the right thing. And I'm not going to just blindly follow your orders anymore. I will have my own life."

He barks out an ugly laugh. "Yes. You *are* on your own. No one will help you now. No one will care about you. And *no one* will want you."

110

"You may be right."

He probably is, and I *do* want to belong somewhere to *someone*. But not at any cost. Swiping the wetness from my face, I turn to leave, to go back to my room and pack the few meager belongings I brought with me—which now amount to all my worldly possessions, I suppose.

Pappa's bitter voice follows me, curling around my ears like black smoke from a trash fire. "You'll be back, you know. Someday you'll fall at my feet and beg me for forgiveness, beg me to take you in again."

I shake my head, not turning back around, not even glancing over my shoulder. There's no point in it. I know what's behind me. My past.

And out there somewhere, far above us on the surface, where the sun shines on the humans and the Elven race alike, is my future.

Somewhere out there—perhaps not too far away—is Nox Knight. I will find him. I will determine the truth about the fate of my beloved childhood friend, my first innocent love.

And if he's the same boy I knew long ago, if he really is alive, then perhaps Pappa is wrong.

Perhaps there *is* someone who will want me. Who will love me for who I was then, for who I really am deep down inside, and for who I will become.

THE END

AFTERWORD

Thank you for reading THE SWAY: A Hidden Saga Companion Novella. I hope you enjoyed it! If you did, would you consider leaving a review at the retailer where you purchased it? Reviews help authors more than you can imagine and help other readers find great new books to read.

If you'd like to know when my next book is available and get inside information and special content, you can sign up for my VIP list at: http://eepurl.com/4lX1f

I'm on Instagram, Facebook, and Twitter. Come find me and let's chat!

You've just read a novella connected to the Hidden Saga. Other books in the series are listed below. I hope you'll love them all!

Hidden Deep

Hidden Heart

Hidden Hope

Hidden Darkness

Hidden Danger

Hidden Desire

Be sure to check out the entire Ancient Court Trilogy and see another side of the Hidden world!

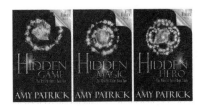

Hidden Game

Hidden Magic

Hidden Hero

AMY PATRICK

Sixteen-year-old Ryann Carroll has just run into the guy who saved her life ten years ago. *You might think she'd be happy to see him again. Not exactly. She's a bit underdressed (as in skinny-dipping) and he's not supposed to exist.*

After her father's affair, all Ryann wants is to escape the family implosion fallout and find a little peace. She also wouldn't mind a first date that didn't suck, but she's determined not to end up like her mom: vulnerable, betrayed, destroyed. Ryann's recently moved into her grandma's house in rural Mississippi, the same place where ten years earlier she became lost in the woods overnight and nearly died.

She's still irresistibly drawn to those woods. There she encounters the boy who kept her from freezing to death that long ago winter night and was nowhere to be seen when rescuers arrived. He's still mysterious, but now all grown-up and gorgeous, too. And the more she's with him, the greater the threat he poses to Ryann's strict policy—never want someone more than he wants you.

Seventeen-year-old Lad knows the law of his people all too well: Don't get careless and Don't get caught. *It's allowed his race to live undetected in this world for thousands of years, mentioned only in flawed and fading folklore. Lad's never been able to forget about Ryann since that night ten years ago. When he sees her again, his fascination re-ignites and becomes a growing desire that tempts him to break all the rules.*

He's not even supposed to talk to a human, much less fall in love with one.

And the timing is atrocious. *The Assemblage is coming, the rift between the Light and Dark is widening. Lad may have to trade his own chance at happiness to keep the humans, especially Ryann, blissfully ignorant and safe.*

What reviewers are saying about HIDDEN DEEP...

"Hidden Deep is a young adult fantasy novel set in steamy rural Mississippi, and the steam spills over to the attraction between Lad and Ryann. The characters are great, and the unique setting comes to life on the pages of this engrossing read" **Misti Pyles- Examiner.com**

"I was immediately drawn to the cool, quiet tranquility of the woods. The details jumped off the page in deep green leaves and cold clear water. Then Lad and Ryann swept me right off my feet... I was glad that I started Hidden Deep on a Friday so that I could read straight through the night into the breaking hours of dawn. It ended way too quickly. I hope the continuation will be out soon. I will be making plans for another Friday night lost in the world of Lad and Ryann." **AJ- Bitten by Books**

"I really got into this story, and every time I reached the end of a chapter I couldn't resist going onto the next one... *Hidden Deep* was a YA fantasy novel like no other. In a world of vampires and demons and witches, a new story with a new mythical background is always welcome. It was a funny, romantic, refreshing read that I'm glad I got to pick up. I'd definitely be interested in reading the rest of this trilogy." **Jessica— The Book Bratz YA book blog**

"I love it when I fall deeper into the story as I move from one chapter to the next. That's what I got here. … as a whole, this book is a delicious read. I actually went back to the first chapter immediately after finishing the epilogue which is EPIC by the way. The cliffhanger left me with my mouth open and ready to reread the whole thing (which I kinda did)." **Lyn Ching, Side B blog**

ABOUT THE AUTHOR

 Amy Patrick is a two-time Golden Heart finalist (2013 and 2014) who writes Contemporary Romance and Young Adult fantasy/paranormal romance. She is the author of the Hidden Saga and the Channel 20 Something series. Living in New England now with her husband and two sons, she actually craves the heat and humidity of Mississippi, where she grew up. She's been a professional singer and news anchor and currently narrates audio books as well as doing other voiceover work.

Contact her at amypatrickbooks@yahoo.com or visit her website www.amypatrickbooks.com.

Be the first to hear about new releases, special pricing, and bonus material by subscribing to Amy's newsletter at http://eepurl.com/4lX1f

Made in the USA
Columbia, SC
10 July 2019